THE REVOLUTION

BOOK 3 OF THE BLOODMOON WARS SERIES (A PARANORMAL SHIFTER ROMANCE SERIES)

SARA SNOW

ELINOR

ear could be crippling. The fear of failing, responsibility, love, and loss could throw someone entirely off their equilibrium.

A drop of blood fell to the ground from the scalp in Cyrus's hand. My stomach clenched at the sight as my eyes stung with tears. We had come so far to rescue Skye, only to discover just a piece of her instead.

Skye can't be dead!

The thought of losing Skye forever paralyzed me. My eyes zeroed in on Cyrus and the clump of Skye's hair. If only I had been able to save her the night the faceless demon abducted her from her bedroom. If only I had been stronger!

No, no! She's not gone!

I shook my head and clenched my fists as Cyrus's brother, Theanos, walked forward and took the small patch of scalp from Cyrus. Cyrus surrendered it without a fight, his face pale with dread. Theanos ripped a large strip from his shirt and wrapped the patch neatly, then tucked it under his shirt. I caught another brief whiff of her scent before tears blurred my vision.

She can't be dead!

Theanos placed his hand on Cyrus's shoulder. "I know how bad this looks, but I can still feel her. That means she's still alive. And as long as I can feel her, I can track her. But before we leave, we need to look around to see what her kidnappers left behind. It looks like they left in a hurry, and they might have forgotten something important."

I glanced behind me at the cell we had walked by, the stench of the mangled bodies inside it still burning my nostrils. My fangs elongated as my eyes turned black, and my fear morphed into something else.

Rage.

Reports indicated that people—supernaturals and humans alike—were disappearing all across the country. Yet we'd only discovered this one location. So how many other lives had come to the same gruesome end as the people in that cell?

At the sound of a door opening, I turned to see Theanos step into the room where Cyrus had found the piece of Skye's scalp. Cyrus remained where he was, his eyes on the ground, and my chest tightened. Skye was the love of his life, his other half.

When he looked up at me, his gray eyes had turned red, reflecting the demon that raged inside him. I met his eyes, and he slowly nodded back at the message they conveyed. We understood each other without the need for words. If Skye died as a result of this, neither one of us would rest until everyone involved in her demise suffered a fate worse than death.

It had been just the three of us—Cyrus, myself, and Skye—since we were children, and even though circumstances were about to separate us, death wasn't supposed to have been one of the reasons. Turning, Cyrus and I entered the room together. Theanos's dragon wings lit up and provided illumination until Cyrus finished lighting the torches on the wall by the door. Only then did I turn around to see what was in the rest of the room.

My brows knitted at the sight before me.

Naked supernaturals hung from the ceiling, suspended from hooks like slabs of beef at the butcher's shop. There were corpses of men, women, and children—some rotting, all covered in cuts and bruises.

"What the hell were they doing in here?" Theanos muttered to himself as he walked further into the room, careful not to touch any of the bodies.

I stepped over a sizable pool of blood while Cyrus remained at the door. There were corpses piled on top of each other in one corner of the room. Clenching my jaw, I walked over to what looked like a large cutting board. There was blood—fresh and dried—on the surface, with multiple tools coated in blood hanging on the wall behind it.

"They left nothing behind but bodies and blood," I growled.

"Look at this," Theanos called from the other end of the room. I made my way through the hanging bodies to find him standing by a long rectangle table. On top was a naked elf, her white hair tangled and dirty.

"What's on her forehead?" I asked, noticing the symbol branded between her eyes.

The symbol was a perfect circle, and inside it was a semicircle facing upwards like a half moon. At the center of the half moon was a line like a pole. It almost looked like an eye.

"I've never seen a symbol like that before," Theanos said after a moment. He leaned over the elf, causing his long blond hair to fall forward to shield his face. "She doesn't smell, which means her body's fresh. Have you ever seen a mark like this, Cyrus?"

"No, I haven't. We need to leave. There is nothing left

here." He took a deep breath, as if bracing himself. "Do you think you can do another spell using Skye's hair?"

Theanos stepped back from the elf's body. "I should be able to, yes."

Before we all turned away, I said, "We should burn everything. We can't leave them like this."

"I have no theories about what was happening here," Theanos said, shaking his head. "There are supernaturals and humans—all dead. Whoever did this hung some bodies from the ceiling and piled others up as if they were trash. Then there's whatever's going on with that elf."

The sound of something shattering echoed through the dark room, and I spun around in fright. The torches by the door went out, plunging the room into darkness. My eyes shifted from green to black as I called on my wolf.

Now I could see just fine, despite the darkness. A body hanging from the ceiling started to swing, then another to the left, and then another, and another.

"Something's in here with us," I whispered, and Cyrus bent down.

"The table," he replied before slowly standing up. "It's broken."

"You mean the table with the elf?" Theanos asked. That was when something wrapped around my ankle and yanked me to the ground.

I screamed, and Cyrus grabbed my arm. I reached down and sliced the vine holding my ankle hostage with my claws. The thick vine retreated as I rose into a fighting stance.

Black claws emerged from Cyrus's fingertips as he stepped forward and sent balls of fire towards the bodies in the ceiling. As flames engulfed the bodies and they fell from their hooks on the ceiling, their dangling legs no longer obstructed our view of the back of the room.

Theanos and I looked at each other with wide eyes when

we saw the empty table where the dead elf with the symbol had been.

"Where is she?" I asked.

Suddenly the elf charged at us from the left, where she'd been hiding behind the bodies still hanging from the ceiling.

The earth beneath our feet trembled, and Theanos was the first to act, his wings flapping forward to create a strong wind that sent the elf flying backward. It also caused more bodies to fall to the ground, allowing us to see better.

Across the room, the naked elf hissed at us. Her milky-blue eyes moved back and forth between us. The previously dull symbol on her forehead had brightened considerably, and I expected her to charge us again. Instead, she let out a thundering cry, and the ground cracked open as hundreds of roots burst from the earth.

Theanos grabbed me around the waist, and both he and Cyrus leaped into the air before the roots could touch us. The sound of high-pitched shrieking met our ears as Cyrus burned the vines, but the more he burned, the more new ones appeared.

"I've never seen an elf with this much power!" Theanos's hold on me tightened while most of the roots conjoined and then pierced through the ceiling above us.

We flew left and right, trying desperately to avoid any falling debris as we tried to escape. I looked down to find the elf skillfully jumping from one root to the next, gaining on us. We emerged into the house above, but the rapidly growing tree was destroying it. Not that it mattered. I doubted anyone planned to return to claim any of the old abandoned houses in this town or the broken furniture now strewn about. It was what had made this place the perfect spot to hide abducted humans and supernaturals.

A chunk of the roof that was stuck to one of the large

branches fell off, crashing into a neighboring house that had its roof intact.

It was common knowledge that elves used earth magic, but like Theanos, I'd never seen an elf with such a powerful command over nature. Once outside, Theanos and I remained on the ground as Cyrus continued to rain fire down onto the tree. However, the branches were now still, and the elf was using the roots to block herself from being burned.

It was a standoff. And because we were in the middle of nowhere, there was no one to help us.

Beside me, Theanos's body changed, tripling in size—thanks to his wings. Unfortunately for me, shifting into either of my wolf forms wouldn't help in this situation.

In my second form, I'd be able to rip the vines apart easily, but they'd return seconds later. The roots couldn't remain our target. We had to kill the elf.

My eyes widened as Cyrus made a quick dive towards the elf, but she used the roots to block him once again.

"I have an idea," I told Theanos.

He looked down at me with black eyes.

I'd seen Cyrus in demon form several times, so I knew the black markings and symbols on his body appeared to move. Since he was half-dragon and half-incubus, Theanos grew a large tail and scales all over his body. I'd never seen him fully transform before, and his changed appearance startled me for a second. But only for a second.

After explaining my plan quickly, I shifted into my second and final form. Whereas my first form—my wolf form—caused my hands to become paws, in my second form, my hands grew bigger and my fingers lengthened. My ears grew pointed and my shoulders hunched forward slightly as my entire body rippled with muscles. My long tail slapped the ground behind me as I stood on two feet instead of on all fours, my white fur flattened to my body.

I climbed onto Theanos's back. He was large and robust enough to carry me in this form, but not for long. We'd have to act quickly, relying on Cyrus to remain a distraction.

A white fog rolled in around us, covering the town and most of the monstrous tree. The mist was being controlled by Theanos, providing us with cover. It caught the elf's attention, but taking her eyes off Cyrus was a mistake. He advanced on her, black mist in the shape of a sword appearing in his hand, allowing him to slice through the roots quickly.

His fist connected with her jaw and sent her flying backwards into the tree as a root pierced his side. That was when Theanos and I acted. We had been waiting patiently in the fog, watching for the slightest opening. The moment she smacked against the tree, dazed, Theanos shot upwards into the sky.

We rose above her and Cyrus within seconds. I untangled my legs from around him as he stopped and turned toward the elf. When he reached around me to grip me, I readied myself. Cyrus and I had done something like this before. The night he took me flying to cheer me up, we had spotted an old man being chased by wraiths. In order to come to the man's rescue from where we were in the air, I stood on Cyrus's back and allowed him to throw me towards the ground.

Theanos did the same thing now, throwing me with all the strength he had and sending me soaring towards the elf. Everything happened so fast, she had no time to escape before we collided, splintering the tree in the process.

My fangs sank into her neck and shoulder. The sound of her bones snapping in my jaws echoed in my ear. I held her

7

close, crushing her body, and a cloud of black smoke caught us inches from the ground.

I clamped down on her neck further and felt her body go limp before Cyrus landed beside us and gradually let us both go. I released the elf, her blood dripping from my mouth. Theanos landed with a thud, and I stood up and shifted back into my human form.

"Uggh! That's nasty," I growled as I wiped the blood on my face away. "It's in my eyes!"

"Here," Cyrus handed me a piece of cloth he'd ripped from his pants, and I hastily took it to wipe my face.

Theanos returned to his usual size with a wide grin on his face. "Damn, that was amazing! I thought your plan was crazy at first, but it worked."

"Step back!" Cyrus shouted, and Theanos and I backed away quickly.

The elf's body below us started to deteriorate from the center of her forehead where the mark was. Within minutes, only her bones remained. We watched in silence, unable to look away. Never had I seen anything like this, and from the looks on Theanos's and Cyrus's faces, they hadn't either.

Theanos was the first to speak. "What the hell just happened? When we first saw her on the table, I was certain she was dead."

Cyrus bent down, his eyes turning red as he looked over the bones on the ground. "Whatever they did in order to make her like this, it involved the use of strong black magic. I can feel the remnants of it, though it's quickly fading now."

"So I'm guessing that mark on her forehead had something to do with her being reanimated?" I finished wiping away the blood on my face, but the smell wouldn't totally disappear without a bath.

In fact, it felt like forever since I'd actually had a proper bath. I'd neglected to take care of myself lately, with all the searching Cyrus and I had done, moving from one place to the next. But that didn't matter right now. Finding Skye was all either of us cared about.

I leaned down to investigate one of the few bones that hadn't fully disintegrated, trying to make sense of what we'd seen. Whatever the mark on her forehead had done to her, I doubted it was with her consent. Finding that dungeon had left us with more questions than answers.

Were there more supernaturals like her out there?

And more importantly, who was behind it all?

2

CYRUS

I stood up and exhaled heavily. "We can't worry about the elf and what they did to her. Not right now. Whoever did this clearly left her behind to kill or delay us, so we need to hurry to find Skye. Whoever has her probably hoped the elf would buy them more time."

Theanos removed the cloth he had stashed away with Skye's hair from under his shirt, and my body grew tense as I nodded towards it.

"Do you think you can do a spell to track her?" I asked him. He nodded as he unraveled the cloth to reveal Skye's black curly hair.

"Yes. Saleem broke the spell blocking her location, and with this amount of hair, I should be able to track her more efficiently now."

"Do it," I told him without hesitation.

He walked away with the hair in his hand, and I looked at Elinor. She was just standing up from where she'd been stooping over the body of the dead elf—what was left of it. I'd never seen anyone rot so quickly. Whatever that symbol had been on her forehead, it not only reanimated her, it boosted her power ten times over.

The faint smell of Skye originating from her hair caused my heart to pound. Now more than ever before, it seemed as if we were in a race against time. I had to believe she was alive. I just had to.

I didn't want to spare even one thought that she might be dead, or I'd lose my mind right here and now. Losing Skye wasn't an option. It just wasn't. She had said she wasn't sure about coming to the Underworld with me, but after this, I'd insist.

I'd be able to protect her there. She'd be safe. Nothing like this would ever happen again, and this would be the last time I'd have to experience the soul-crushing ache that threatened to consume me now.

I looked up at the deep orange sky as the sun began to set. So much time had already passed since we arrived in this place.

"We'll find her and Ms. Clementine." Elinor's words were soft, but her heart was thumping as fast as mine was. "They have to be okay."

"They are." I inhaled deeply as Theanos's chanting met my ears.

An image of Ms. Clementine dressing my wounds the first night I had arrived at the pack house resurfaced in my mind, and my chest tightened. My own mother was a selfish and heartless demon.

Ms. Clementine was . . . is nothing like her.

She'd been grateful to me for saving her only daughter and hadn't hesitated to offer a demon child safety within her home. I had so much to thank her for. I just hoped she and Skye weren't separated. In the heat of the moment, I had only taken something belonging to Skye to help track her, assuming they'd be together.

In the end, if we found Skye and not Ms. Clementine, we'd just have to keep looking. No one was going home until both women were safe.

"I've got her location, but it isn't fixed. They're taking her somewhere. We need to go now. Prepare yourselves for a fight." Theanos's wings spread as he prepared for flight.

Elinor climbed onto my back quickly, and we took to the sky with Theanos leading the way. The wound in my side had already healed itself, and I was ready to face any other supernatural waiting for us. Because I knew getting Skye back wouldn't be easy. I doubted the elf was the only surprise Skye's captors had in store for us.

"Keep an eye out," I yelled to Theanos up ahead. "That elf might not be the only threat."

Depending on what kind of reanimated supernatural we ran into, we'd likely be slowed down yet again. A lightning bolt struck inches away from Theanos, throwing him to the side. Elinor's arm tightened around my neck as I dove towards the forest below us, and Theanos followed suit.

If we ran through the forest on foot, it would slow us down considerably, but flying above the forest left us with no cover. I sensed the same power as I had felt from the reanimated elf vibrating through the air as we landed.

"I feel it now," Theanos said under his breath as I lowered Elinor to the ground. I scanned the surrounding forest.

Three figures stepped out of the shadows and my jaws clenched. I watched, wary and ready, as a witch moved toward us, small bolts of lightning dancing on her fingertips.

On one side of her was a werewolf, and on the other, a male elf. All of them sported the same symbol I'd seen on the last elf on various parts of their naked bodies.

This was going to be a problem. One supercharged supernatural had been enough, and now we faced three. I glanced to my right and saw Theanos shift into his demon form, his tail flicking wildly behind him. Elinor was now in her second wolf form on my left, her pure white fur standing out against the dark forest in the background.

The werewolf in front of us howled to the sky, his fists clenched at his sides. Elinor growled and bared her fangs.

"Fight to kill," I said gruffly as the bones and tendons in my body broke and stretched, forcing my body to grow larger. "We don't have time to waste."

Beside me, Elinor hunched forward, her large paw-like hands opening and closing as her razor-sharp claws elongated. I sensed the staggering power radiating from her body, and I smiled inwardly, thankful she was on my side.

"Elinor, I'm talking to you. Don't hold back."

A soft growl rumbled in her chest in acknowledgment as she glanced at me and then back at her opponent.

I'd often noticed that there were two sides to Elinor—the pack leader's daughter, and the Alpha she was born to become. As the pack leader's daughter, she held herself back —almost involuntarily—after a lifetime of being told that a female couldn't lead, couldn't have power.

But Elinor had always been more than just a female first-born. The Werewolf Guard examination offered her the chance to finally break free from those chains. But after the death of her friend during the trials, she acted more distrustful of her own power than ever.

And not being able to save Skye had only increased that doubt. She had so much going on in her life . . . like her father arranging to marry her off to a wolf who wasn't her mate just as she finally realized she had feelings for a vampire. She was stressed beyond belief . . . and I hated it.

I'd glimpsed the confident and stubborn wolf I'd always known back at Saleem's bar when she had jumped from the roof of the building to save a woman from two vampires.

And I'd seen her again just a few minutes ago, when she had devised the plan with Theanos to kill the elf.

If she was serious about becoming a bounty hunter, she'd have to stop doubting herself. She had incredible power. She just needed to trust herself enough to use it.

Theanos made the first move, charging at the elf before he had time to build a root barrier like the previous one had. I let the discomfort of shifting roll over me and focused on the witch before me. My power was pulsating within my veins, desperate for release, and everyone who stood in the way of me finding Skye and Ms. Clementine would feel my wrath.

Elinor

*L*ightning bolts directed at Cyrus along with the balls of fire he was using to retaliate lit up the forest around us. But I couldn't focus on them—I had a supercharged werewolf to deal with.

He was massive, standing at least a foot taller than me, but I growled low, reminding myself who I was. I chanted it in my head like a spell . . . *I am Elinor Blackwood, firstborn to Alpha Grayson Blackwood, and I have power. This wolf is no match for me.*

He came charging towards me first, his enormous feet stomping on the ground. Widening my stance, I readied myself and opened my arms wide. My legs were rooted to the ground, so when the werewolf smacked into me, he barely pushed me back at all. I felt his claws sink into my back, but I wrapped my arms around him and squeezed. He might be bigger than I was, but that didn't mean he was stronger.

The sound of snapping bones echoed through the night along with the wolf's whimpers, but I was forced to release him when his fangs missed my throat by an inch. The second I released him, he charged at me again, and this time when we collided, he seemed stronger. And either his broken bones had already healed, or he felt no pain from them anymore.

What the hell is he?

We fell to the ground in a tangled mess of fangs, claws, and snapping jaws. The more we fought, the stronger he became, almost as if he was feeding off my strength. We rolled over, and I got the upper hand, quickly grabbing his open mouth with both hands. I needed to end this fight —pronto.

I winced as his arms clawed at me. Still, I forced my weight down onto him, trapping him beneath me, then pulled his mouth open until his jawbone snapped and his skull shattered.

He fell lifeless, and I hurriedly got off him as his body swiftly deteriorated, starting from the symbol on his left shoulder.

My wolf raged inside me. But I wasn't angry at the were-wolf. None of this was his fault. Someone killed him, then reanimated him. No, I was incensed at whoever had done this to him. I stepped back as he was reduced to bones, my blood boiling.

"Elinor!"

I spun towards Cyrus just in time to see a bolt of light-ning coming towards me. I stepped to the side, narrowly missing being hit in the chest, but the bolt struck my arm. Pain rolled up to my shoulder as I flew backward, colliding with a tree.

A roar filled the air, and a burst of black energy engulfed us all. I blinked rapidly to clear my vision, but I knew who that energy belonged to. Though I was still dazed by the attack, I realized Cyrus was losing control. My close call with the lightning bolt probably pushed him over the edge.

An intense gust of wind from out of nowhere caused the trees to blow wildly. I held my burned hand to my chest, waiting for my quick werewolf healing to kick in. But the damage was too severe, and the pain was paralyzing. I involuntarily shifted back into my human form, just thankful my spelled clothing didn't cover my wounded arm.

I knew keeping this Werewolf Guards uniform was a good idea.

When my vision finally cleared, I realized Cyrus had taken to the sky, and the strong wind I felt was being created by his flapping wings. But when the wind turned into scorching heat, my heart stopped beating for a second as I watched his entire body morph into blue flames.

At first, I thought maybe the witch had cast a spell, but Cyrus stretched out his arms and sent a shaft of blue flames hurtling towards the witch. Her scream filled the forest as the fire consumed her. In mere moments, it reduced her to ashes.

I couldn't look away as Cyrus hovered above the ground, his wings and entire body in flames. He dipped, falling to the ground, but caught himself. As he landed, he covered his face with his hands. Theanos appeared behind the elf, who'd been briefly transfixed by Cyrus's blue flames, and wrapped his large tail around him so he couldn't move. Then he reached around the elf to take hold of his throat, his clawed fingers digging into the elf's flesh.

The elf bared his teeth, and the roots surrounding them both flew about wildly.

"Stop!" Theanos told him.

Elves were usually calm beings, so seeing one so agitated and violent was really strange. This one was acting just like the female elf we had fought in the basement. Thankfully, this elf seemed to listen to Theanos, and the roots that had been wildly flying around them stopped.

"Cyrus!" Theanos called. "Cyrus!"

"Cyrus!" I said, and his hand finally fell from his face. He looked my way, and amid the blue flames, red eyes peered down at me. "It's over. Remember her, Cyrus. Focus on Skye."

The flames around him slowly shrank in size. I got up, wincing at the pain in my arm, and forced myself to walk over to him. His shoulders were rising and falling rapidly.

Did he just discover a new power?

He straightened the moment I got to his side. He looked my way, his eyes still red, but he nodded at me reassuringly, letting me know he was fine, that he'd found his control again.

"Who are you?" We both turned to see Theanos tightening his tail around the elf. "Who did this to you? Can you speak?"

The elf's eyes were unnaturally pale like the other reanimated supernaturals we had encountered, and I sighed. We wouldn't get any answers from him. I doubted the elf even understood what Theanos was saying. The mark on his left pec burned brighter, and suddenly, a root exploded out from the ground and pierced the elf's chest.

Luckily, Theanos had released the elf the moment the root appeared. When the elf's body fell to the ground and deteriorated, we looked at each other in confusion. I exhaled heavily as the tingling sensation in my arm continued. '

"I didn't imagine that just now, right? He killed himself?" I asked. "I've had enough of this. We need to find Skye and get the hell out of here." Cyrus turned away, and I narrowed my eyes at him as he reached up and pressed a finger to his temple. "What just happened to you?"

"I lost control, that's all," he mumbled in response. Theanos and I shared a look of concern. "I'm fine. Really."

"Uhh . . . you don't look fine, Cyrus. Was that the first time that's happened to you? You had blue flames."

"No, it wasn't the first time. My father has blue flames," he growled. "That was just the first time in ages that I've had to use them. I forcefully broke the block I'd placed on my powers, so I have a raging headache. But it'll be okay."

"Is there anything else I don't know about my best friend? Are you going to . . . I don't know, grow a second head? Why haven't I heard about these blue flames before?"

He turned to face me, scowling. "Because they're destructive. It's a power I haven't been able to get complete control of."

Theanos cleared his throat. "We need to go."

I frowned at the look of panic on his face. "What's wrong?"

His wings unfolded from his back. "We need to go now. I can still feel Skye, but my hold on her is fading."

Cyrus's wings unfolded as well, his red eyes burning brighter. "What does that mean?"

Theanos's next words made me forget all about the pain in my arm. "It means she's dying."

3

ELINOR

*T*heanos suggested we run instead of fly. If any other supernaturals hidden within the forest spotted us in the air, it could delay us again, and we might not find Skye in time.

The longer we traveled without finding her, the more panicked I felt. Dawn was drawing closer, and if her energy was fading—if she was dying—every second counted. I quickly sent a prayer to the Goddess to keep her alive until we found her.

Suddenly, Theanos halted and began walking in a circle. He hissed, then a frantic expression appeared on his face. I clenched my jaw, hoping against hope that he'd found something, until he started running again.

Cyrus and I followed after him, and a few minutes later, Theanos pointed at something—at someone—lying on the forest floor in the distance.

"Skye?" Cyrus yelled, flying over to her while Theanos and I followed on foot.

I fell to my knees beside her, and her eyes cracked open just a little.

"Stop!" Her frail voice met my ears. "It's a trap."

"We're surrounded," Theanos hissed.

"By how many?" I asked.

"I count seven," he answered.

I looked back down at Skye. Even though we were facing another fight, I smiled, thanking the Goddess for keeping my friend safe. But I was heartbroken at finding her in this state. She was covered in dirt and blood, and a section of her scalp, which was undoubtedly what we'd found earlier, hadn't healed yet. One of her eyes looked slightly swollen, and she looked worn out, which would make the healing process even slower.

I wiped away a streak of dirt from her cheek. "Where is your mother?"

Her face twisted as if she was in pain, and Cyrus scanned her body frantically. "Skye? What's wrong?"

"T-they—" She stuttered as the sound of rattling in the bushes grew closer. "They made . . . me . . . watch them . . ." Tears ran down her cheeks. ". . . kill her."

No! Goddess no!

I hung my head and growled low, the pain of losing yet another member of my pack rapidly eating away at my insides. I shook my head, unable to believe Ms. Clementine was dead. Skye's soft whimper broke my heart, and on the other side of her, Cyrus clenched and unclenched his fists, his blood dripping to the forest floor as his nails pierced his palms.

The darkness of the night faded away as morning took its place, but this day was starting off as horrible as the last.

"What did they do with her body?" Cyrus asked. Skye didn't respond, and I could sense her heartbeat slowing. Cyrus moved forward to gently pick her up. Skye's thin arm dangled lifelessly. "Theanos, take her and go. You fly faster than I do."

Theanos turned around to look at Cyrus with puzzlement. "Okay, but you're coming, right? We can fly out of here together."

"No," Cyrus answered, the word leaving his lips as a growl. I saw the thirst for blood in his eyes, and I shared it. "They'll only follow us. I'll stay behind and delay them while you get the girls out of here."

"The girls? Is there another girl here besides Skye and me? Because I'm not leaving."

"This isn't up for debate, Elinor."

"No, it's not. Because I'm not leaving! We all lost her, damn it!" My voice cracked as my eyes turned black. "Ms. Clementine was . . . a mother to us all. Not to mention, what kind of friend would I be if I left you here to face the rest of these reanimated supernaturals alone? Give it up, Cyrus. I'm not going anywhere!"

In his arms, Skye whimpered yet again and more tears leaked from her eyes. Despite being too weak to talk anymore, her tears spoke volumes. Seeing her pain ripped my heart apart all over again.

I'm so sorry.

My mother's face flashed in my mind, and I clenched my fists. I couldn't imagine the pain I'd feel if I lost her. Regretfully, Skye now knew that pain all too well.

Ms. Clementine didn't deserve what they did to her, and neither any of the supernaturals currently headed our way. But all we could do for them was release them from this never-ending torture.

Theanos took Skye from Cyrus. "I'll take her to the bar and come back."

Cyrus nodded as a mighty howl echoed through the forest. A werewolf burst from the bushes . . . and was immediately engulfed in flames, the first to taste Cyrus's wrath before he took to the sky. I released the pain burning in my veins and howled to the sky, loud and mournfully. My bones snapped and readjusted, but I ignored them as I shifted into my first form.

I shook my body just as an elf appeared from the darkness. But I was ready for him.

Cyrus and I fought viciously against the supernaturals that kept pouring out of the forest. The reality of our situation hit me when I was quickly forced to shift into my final form, only to then become caught up in vines covered in spikes. Although my final form allowed me more freedom and a better ability to fight in hand-to-hand combat, it couldn't help me now. It felt like needles were piercing my entire body.

Cyrus created a circle of fire around us, quickly freeing me, and I shifted into my human form. "We can't fight them alone! We're fighting too many different powers at once!"

The flames around us suddenly parted, and a witch with red hair stepped into our circle. The flames Cyrus had created to protect us flickered, then seemed to fall under her control. Waving her arm, she sent them rushing towards us. Cyrus stepped in front of me, his arms outstretched. The veins in his arms bulged as he fought to regain control of the flames before they consumed us both. Opening his arms wide, he separated the flames, engulfing an elf on his left and another witch on his right.

But we were far from winning this fight.

When more supernaturals appeared, I yelled, "Use your blue flames!"

"I can't. If I lose control, this entire forest will burn down!"

Thunder rumbled above us, and despite the bright orange sky, a sudden downpour of rain soaked us through. But it didn't stop our battle. Cyrus and I continued to fight, though it soon became obvious that we were outmatched.

"Run!" Cyrus yelled, but as I turned to do just that, lightning struck the ground in front of me, missing me by an inch.

"I think you should stay," a voice said. And suddenly, all the supernaturals went still.

Cyrus and I paused, but that brief distraction allowed roots to spring up from the ground and quickly trap us both. I winced as multiple thorns embedded themselves in my flesh. If I moved so much as a finger, the thorns went deeper.

"I would advise against burning those vines and freeing yourself, Cyrus." A cloaked figure appeared before us. "Look around you. You're outnumbered, ten to two."

"Who are you? How do you know my name?"

"Oh, we got a lot of information from . . . what was her name again? Clementine, right? I think her name was Clementine. Yes, yes, it was."

How dare you say her name!

I growled, my wolf needing to see this creature—whatever it was—beheaded. "Who are you? Where is she?" I yelled.

The cloaked figure stepped closer to me, and I realized he had no scent. "Call me Arden. And you must be the white wolf, Elinor. I would ask my companion—" He nodded to an elf standing behind him. "—to release you and let you shift, but I don't think that would be a good idea."

"Why not? I'm a darling. I don't bite, really."

He stepped closer to me, then stopped. Even at this distance, I couldn't see a face beneath the large hood of his cloak. "So, you're a female firstborn? I expected more."

"Oh really? Because you are exactly what I expected—a piece of scum. What did you do to these supernaturals?"

"Listen, you two got your little wolf friend back, right? Great. Now I'd suggest you stay out of business that doesn't concern you."

23

"You're joking, right? Everyone we know is in danger because of you. You murdered an innocent woman—a woman we loved—and for that, I promise you, you're going to burn in hell."

"Well, you see, the problem is . . ." He pulled his cloak off and rolled his shoulders. "I've already been there."

After getting a good look at him, I believed him.

He wore dark gray pants and no shirt. His chest was bare except for a symbol, which spanned from his collarbone down to his waist and looked totally different than the one carved into the other supernaturals. His arms, legs, and fingers all appeared to have been sewn on, and much of his skin was made up of different skin tones. His face, neck, and chest were the only parts that shared the same pale complexion.

"So, were you born like that, or . . ." I drawled, and beside me, Cyrus chuckled.

"Funny. But no. I was reborn." Arden's green eyes narrowed. The stitches around them made it look as if his eyes had been removed and replaced, and it was hard to tell what species he belonged to. Especially because he had no scent. He looked at Cyrus, and then at me. "Much the same way these supernaturals were reborn. My master has plans. Plans for this world and these supernaturals . . . I am needed."

I growled. "And what plans might those be, huh?"

"What did your master do to them?" Cyrus asked. I tried to look at him, but turning my head caused a thorn to sink deeper into my neck.

I felt blood running down my body from multiple puncture wounds, the smell of it rich in the air. Our only option now was to keep Arden talking until Theanos returned, but I doubted he had even reached the bar yet.

We were caught.

I stopped moving and focused on Arden as he walked

away, coming to stand beside an elf. He patted her cheek gently, only she neither blinked nor moved. She just stared dead ahead, like a doll waiting to be played with.

"What did your master do to them?" Cyrus asked again.

"You won't get any answers from me on that. But you should know, they are already dead, so there is no saving them," Arden answered. "Now they are merely puppets. There are more of them than you can imagine, and they only have one purpose."

It was as I had expected. The elf in the dungeon had definitely been dead when we were standing over her. The mark was likely what had reanimated her. But why? What purpose would these poor souls serve?

"Where is she?" I glared at him. "Where is my friend's mother? Give her body to us."

"I don't know what they did with her body."

"You were among the first, weren't you?" Cyrus guessed, and Arden frowned. "You were among the first that your master experimented on. That's why you don't look like the others. You've retained your consciousness."

"Right you are. We weren't murdered like these stupid things. There are others like me who were enhanced."

I didn't know why I expected him to hold any sympathy for the supernaturals whose lives—and afterlives—had been destroyed, but I did. He was speaking so casually about what his masters had done to these innocents. He didn't even seem to care that he, himself, had been turned into a doll—one that had been pulled apart and sewn back together, and poorly at that.

The longer he spoke, the more I wanted to rip his throat out. His eyes changed from green to black, revealing he was, in fact, a demon. Or was he, if indeed his eyes had been replaced? And now that I thought about it, we hadn't encountered any vampires or demons with the same mark as these reanimated supernaturals yet.

Did that mean vampires or demons were behind all of this?

"It took a while for my master to find the right method—one that would offer absolute obedience."

"Why? And who the hell is your master?" I asked.

The corner of his mouth curved in a smirk. "I guess you'll find out soon enough, right?" He held his hands out, his palms facing upward, and his smirk turned into a look filled with venom. "Then again, maybe you two won't be around to see it."

On his left hand, lightning danced across his fingers as if he were a witch. On the right, black mist, like that belonging to a demon, appeared.

So I was right. There's no way to tell if he was originally a demon or a witch. Whatever experiment was done to him has somehow given him the ability to use powers from multiple supernaturals.

The mark on his chest glowed, and his eyes rolled backwards. "This world needs cleansing. It needs a new ruler, and it will receive one. So far, you two are the only ones to get this far. But this is where it ends."

His eyes opened, and a lightning bolt from his hand struck the ground in front of me. I called on my wolf, wincing as the thorns sunk deeper into my skin as I tried to shift, but I refused to die without a fight. Cyrus's words from earlier suddenly filled my mind. I couldn't hold back. I'd done enough of that. And the last time, my friend had died horribly because of it.

If Meeka had been here now, she wouldn't have let a few thorns keep her trapped. She had believed in her strength as an Alpha-born.

My body shook as my bones began to break. After

Meeka's death and my father's betrayal, I'd lost my drive to be a warrior. I'd allowed myself to be bullied into living with the choices others forced on me.

But not anymore.

"You killed someone I loved," Cyrus roared, the rage in his voice echoing the wrath building inside me. I howled loudly, creating a backdrop for the words he threw at Arden like weapons. "You hurt the only woman on this earth who has kept me from becoming my father. I'll drag you to hell myself if I have to!"

Black smoke rose from the roots holding me, and I watched as they began to rot. Arden's smug expression vanished as he looked first at me, and then at Cyrus.

The mark on his chest burned brighter, and the supernaturals surrounding us moved as if to attack us again. "It doesn't matter what you do, Cyrus." He closed his eyes, and his mark pulsated. "I'll destroy everything within a hundred miles. You can't stop us. You can't stop me!"

I broke free as soon as the roots holding me rotted away, but an elf with the mark branded onto his cheek tackled me before I had time to think. We tumbled to the ground. I forced my strength and power into my legs, then kicked him off me, sending his body flying into the trees. I jumped to my feet and looked around.

Three witches were holding their hands up to the sky, causing lightning to rain down on Cyrus. Cyrus was blinded by his rage, the black mist around him morphing into blue flames. Those flames were the only advantage we had, but they came with a terrible risk.

"Don't!"

Cyrus's body stiffened for a second, as if realizing how close he was to losing control. He allowed his flames to die away but continued to stalk Arden, who was being shielded by witches. The puppet (that was the only way I could think of him) was chanting soft words I didn't understand, and the energy in the air started to feel warm. If he was some type of walking bomb, we'd all be done for.

Cyrus dodged a lightning bolt as I shifted into my human form to battle another elf. I needed the agility of my human form without the body mass of my final wolf form. My claws slit the elf's throat, and I continued moving towards Arden with Cyrus, but I paused when he jumped back. Something flashed before him in a blur, and an elf to his left was beheaded.

The surrounding supernaturals started falling like leaves from a tree, and I turned around quickly, trying to figure out what was happening.

"None of you will survive!" Arden roared as his eyes opened, and steam rose off his body.

The chaos around us came to a stop as a hand appeared through his chest from behind, and his black eye reverted to green. Blood spilled from his lips as he looked down at the clawed hand poking through his chest.

The pulsing mark on his chest faded, and the clawed hand retracted. Arden fell to the ground, his lifeless body hitting the forest floor hard, adding to the pile of dead bodies around us.

For a moment, I thought maybe Theanos had returned. Then a familiar scent drifted to my nostrils, and my skin grew warm as I found myself unable to look away from the man who now stood in front of us.

"H-how?" I stuttered before Cyrus moved in front of me protectively.

Will wiped the blood coating his hand on his pants, then stepped forward and into the sun. "Looks like I got here just in time."

4

ELINOR

*C*yrus glared at Will as I stood frozen in shock. Will, a vampire, was standing in the sun as if it was nothing. There wasn't even steam rising from his body.

He was just standing there, staring at us.

Was this even Will, or merely someone who looked exactly like him? I couldn't muster the words to ask as he stepped forward but stopped when Cyrus pointed a finger at him.

"Stay right where you are. What the hell are you?"

Will sighed. "I think you and I went through this before. You know, when you found me in the woods with Elinor?"

This man looked like Will, spoke like Will, and had Will's memories. But how could he possibly be Will?

"How are you out during the daytime?" Cyrus demanded.

Ignoring Cyrus, Will's intense blue eyes slid to me. I read the remorse in them, and my chest tightened painfully. How could he have kept a secret like this from me?

Then again, why was I surprised? He'd been the secretive type since the first moment we met. But this, *this* was unimaginable. A vampire who could walk in the sun . . .

"Elinor?"

I shook my head at him.

"I can explain."

Cyrus lowered the hand he had raised at Will, though he still kept me behind him. "Then do that. How are you able to be out in the daylight?"

Will didn't answer right away. I couldn't look away when his blue eyes pierced into mine. A part of me wanted to run to him, desperate for him to hold me in his arms once again. But another part of me was telling me to remain right where I was.

Looking at Will, I wondered if I really knew him as well as I thought I had. Because right now, he seemed like a complete stranger.

In the sunlight, his dark hair seemed even more beautiful. His blue eyes shone, though they still held the same intensity. And his skin was a stunning porcelain cream, not as pale as it was when he was in cold-blooded vampire-mode.

I needed to understand how his heart could be beating now, but other times, still and lifeless. Why was he so unlike a typical vampire?

"I kept my soul after I was changed centuries ago," Will admitted.

I stepped out from behind Cyrus, needing to hear every word of this explanation.

Will offered us a small smile. "I have a beating heart, I have warm blood in my veins, and I can walk in the sun because I'm not dead and soulless like other vampires."

"That's impossible," Cyrus murmured.

"Yet here I stand." Will's eyes drifted to me. "I wouldn't lie to you—I never have. I'm the same person you've always known. I'm just able to walk in the sun the way you do. I might have secrets, but I've never lied. I didn't tell you about it because it's not something I talk about. If word got out that there was a vampire that didn't have to go into stasis during the daylight, the supernatural community would panic."

"They'd either assume that there are more vampires like you who can walk in the sun or that vampires, as a species, are evolving," Cyrus rubbed at his chin. "Are there any more like you?"

"No. I'm the only one of my kind. I'm a vampire, yes, but also . . . not."

I could almost feel the grief in his words and realized I had heard that tone in his voice before—when he'd told me he understood what it was like to have a life you didn't want forced on you.

While he was entitled to his privacy, I wanted to tell him that he could have told me. He should have known that I wouldn't have revealed his secrets. We'd tried and failed to grow closer, and each time it felt like we were finally getting the chance, another wall arose between us. Looking at him now, I wanted to run to him.

Instead, I kept my fists clenched behind my back and stood my ground.

After the date we'd had in the dragon's forest, I thought we'd forged a genuine connection. It felt like we'd taken a huge step forward, and I'd been elated that he had finally been opening up to me. But apparently, he held back this big secret the whole time.

I felt angry and frustrated that what was between us was so stagnant.

"How?" I finally spoke. "How were you able to keep your soul? If it happened to you, why can't it happen to anyone who's been turned?"

"It just . . . can't." He exhaled heavily and looked up at the sky for a moment. A pang of worry ran through me. He'd been out in the sun now for a while with no consequences.

But I couldn't help fearing that at any moment, he would burst into flames.

I bit down on my lip, trying to focus on the issue on hand —not my feelings for him.

"No other vampire can gain my ability because . . ." He took another deep breath. "I'm of royal blood. That's how I got the power to begin with."

My face scrunched up with confusion. "What? You're royalty? What are you saying?"

"You're a General," Cyrus mumbled, obviously realizing something I hadn't figured out yet. What did it mean to be a vampire General? "If you gained the ability to walk in the sun after you were turned, that means you were . . ."

"Yes." Will exhaled with a nod.

I looked from one man to the other. "What the hell are you two talking about? Can both of you speak in code some other time?"

"He's of royal blood, Elinor. He's a General, a leader among the vampires." At my continued look of confusion, Cyrus rubbed his temple with growing frustration. "Elinor, what this means is that Will is the son of the Vampire Queen." He let out a soft chuckle. "Who'd ever believe it? An Alpha-born werewolf has been dating a vampire prince."

Will

$\mathcal{I}$ hadn't wanted Elinor to find out the truth this way. I had planned to tell her I was a prince among my kind in my own time and after the upheaval of her friend Skye's abduction had been resolved. Our afternoon in the dragon forest solidified my decision to be with her. She brought wonder back into the life of a vampire who had lived for far too long.

The way she admired the creatures in the forest that day had reminded me of the curiosity and appreciation for life I used to have but had long since forgotten.

When I first met her, I craved her, but mainly to satisfy my hunger. She had presented me with a challenge: prey who wouldn't be like the others, who would have fought me to the death. And I wanted that challenge. When we met that evening so long ago, I'd sensed not only her fear but also her curiosity. I'd found it strangely appealing. Instead of running from me, she'd stood her ground, and it made me desperate to learn how her blood would taste. I had wondered if I would be able to taste her naïve courage there.

But when I saw her attacked by those hairless and blood-thirsty Bleeders, a different sensation washed over me—a desire to protect her. After seeing how bravely she fought, I recognized an undeniable spark, a fire within her that couldn't be contained. And from then on, I was like a moth to her flame.

Holding off on telling her I could walk in the sun wasn't a decision I'd made because I didn't trust her. The right moment to tell her just never presented itself, and telling her about my ability would've forced me to explain how I'd gained it.

I would've had to admit that my mother was the Vampire Queen. The last thing I wanted to do was chase her away, and I knew that information was likely to do it. There was a time when I'd hunted the other beings of this earth without restraint or remorse. Even my own kind had feared me. But I grew tired of being cruel, and I soon became an outcast among my kind. They said I wasn't one of them. And I certainly wasn't a human either.

Many people still feared me, but only one person loved

me—my mother. Although I recognized what she felt for me wasn't really love. It was more that she took pride in the fact that I was her son, that my gifts made me special among vampires and I belonged to her.

Yet Elinor didn't discriminate against me, even after she realized I was a vampire. To her, I was just a man. She saw my red eyes and felt my cool skin, and still, she was more curious than afraid. She didn't run away from me . . . even though she really should have.

Because of who I was, our friendship posed an even greater risk of starting a war between her kind and mine. Still, a part of me couldn't be without her snappy, I'm-doing-whatever-I-want attitude. She had the ambition to go after the life she wanted, the drive to follow her dreams regardless of what others thought.

Her inner light brightened the dark world I'd lived in for centuries, and I couldn't be without her.

Will

After we returned to the bar, Elinor and Cyrus went in search of Skye, who was being treated for her injuries by Saleem. When Elinor learned her friend would recover, I heard her frantic heartbeat finally slow down.

During the entire journey back, she hadn't said a word to me, and I couldn't blame her. I glanced at her sitting across the room, watching as Saleem cast a spell on Arden's severed head, and I could tell she was trying to not look my way. I didn't regret following her after they'd left the bar looking for Skye. I had kept my distance, not wanting to interfere . . . until I had to. If I hadn't acted when I did, they would have died.

I understood that she felt betrayed. I also understood her feeling hesitant about me now that she'd found out who I really was. When I learned she was the firstborn daughter of an Alpha, I felt the same way. I had planned to stay away from her, but alas, I couldn't.

Even with all the risks our friendship would bring about, I found my way to her, night after night. I feared losing her, so I kept my true identity a secret. But now it looked like I would lose her anyway. I could almost see the wall growing between us, a barrier I'd been trying to knock down, bit by bit, each time we spoke.

She looked my way but turned away again when she saw me watching her. I sighed. I craved her still, but now I desired all of her. For always.

For now, while her friend was recovering, I wouldn't pressure her. From what I'd heard, Skye's mother had been killed. That had to have been a punch in the gut to both Cyrus and Elinor. I knew how close they all were.

I wished I could comfort her, but I knew I was the last person she wanted to speak to right now.

Skye had fallen asleep, but Cyrus wasn't leaving her side. When we'd arrived, he'd given Arden's head to Saleem, and now the rest of us were all sitting in her office, listening as she interrogated the severed head. I'd seen more substantial black magic users over the years, but Saleem was skilled enough to pull off a spell this strong.

"All . . . all I've heard . . . heard w-was his voice. He never revealed his face a-and he . . . he moved f-from one location t-to the next often." Arden's lips moved slowly, his words chopped.

Saleem continued to wiggle her fingers, sending blue lines of energy extending from her fingertips to his temples. "You've been kidnapping people from their homes and murdering them without even knowing who you were doing it for?" Her finger twitched as she waited for a response.

"Yes . . . y-yes . . . It was my purpose."

"What is the symbol that is branded on the supernaturals, the one that controls them?" Scarlet asked, leaning against the wall to my left.

As a succubus, Scarlet, with her long red hair, was striking. But she still wasn't as beautiful as Elinor. Both she and Theanos had been sending me odd looks, which I interpreted as either curiosity or confusion about what they had just learned about me.

"My m-m-master created i-it. It reanimates the dead, but p-places them . . . under my master's c-control."

"Is your master a witch?" Theanos asked.

"I d-don't know."

Scarlet groaned with frustration. "Were you working alone?"

"No. T-There were two others with me, from t-the first . . . first trials my m-master did."

"Were you the one who killed Ms. Clementine?" Elinor asked.

Arden paused, his pale dead eyes moving frantically from side to side. "No."

Then Saleem decided to go for broke. "Give us a location where other supernaturals are being held," she commanded.

Arden's forehead creased like he was in pain. I knew this particular spell was painful. Arden didn't have a body, but the pain receptors in his brain were being manipulated by Saleem while she stimulated the areas of his brain responsible for memories.

"I-It h-h-hurts. Please."

I glanced at Elinor and watched as her face scrunched up at Arden's words. I knew she was feeling bad about doing this to him. He was cruel and deserved to die. And if she'd had the chance, I was certain she would've quickly put him out of his misery.

But this was torture—something she vehemently disapproved of. It was necessary, and she knew that, too. That was something I loved about her. She was fierce but had morals.

Love?

I frowned as the word echoed in my mind, and I looked away. Love? Did I love her? She'd gotten under my skin, but was it more than that? I'd fight for her, I'd do anything to keep her safe, I'd revealed my secret to save her . . . and I'd ignored the possibility of a war just to be with her.

I groaned and pinched the bridge of my nose. "Fuck."

"Will, is there a problem?" Saleem asked.

My hand fell away from my face. "No."

She nodded, then got back to business. "Give me a location," she urged again, and Arden finally muttered directions that Theanos quickly jotted down.

Saleem sighed loudly as her office door opened, and Cyrus walked in. He entered slowly, his hand in his pockets. While he looked calm on the outside, I knew his need for revenge was eating away at him. He was a fearless man—truly a Demon King's son—and he reminded me of myself. He showed restraint as he walked around and did his best to hide the blood lust brewing within him.

"Is she speaking yet?" Elinor asked him, and he shook his head.

Then he turned to look at the severed head. "Can he feel pain?" he asked Saleem.

She broke the spell connecting her to Arden. "This spell was painful, yes, but needless torture will get us nowhere. We got very little information from Arden. He knew less about what was going on than I had imagined. However, he did give us a location."

"Then show—" he demanded, but Saleem held her hand up to silence him.

"I will not. Ground yourself, Cyrus. Losing control won't solve anything."

"She was my mother, too!" Cyrus's voice vibrated the glasses on the shelves behind Saleem. "And they took her from us!"

To Saleem's credit, she didn't even blink at his outburst. "I know," she replied, her voice low.

Elinor looked away, her heartbeat spiking, and my hand twitched with the need to touch her, to comfort her. Cyrus's hands shook at his sides, and my chest tightened as Elinor hung her head and let out a small sob.

I didn't know the woman they'd lost, but Elinor's pain awakened something in me I hadn't felt in a long time—a thirst for blood, a need to rip the world apart to rid her of anyone or anything that was causing her pain. Only once before had I cared for another, but it had been nothing like this.

Cyrus's eyes grew red with tears, and he turned and left as Elinor sobbed quietly. She got up and rushed from the room with her head down. My body acted on its own and I reached out to her, but she growled deep, her eyes changing to black, and I froze.

Then she stormed from the room, and I remained where I stood for a mere second before hissing and rushing after her. She was in pain, no doubt on the verge of exploding with everything that had happened in the last few weeks. But I knew if I left now, the issue between us would only end up tied to the rage she felt for the people who took her friend.

"Elinor!" She kept walking down the hall. I moved forward quickly, grabbing her arm and pulling her into a room. "Wait."

"Get off me!" she cried.

I released her arm. "Sorry, I just . . ."

"What? You just what, Will? What the hell just happened?"

Her cheeks were slick with tears, and I didn't understand the sudden ache in my chest at the sight of them. Her eyes were filled with so much pain . . .

"I'm sorry." That was all I could say—I had no excuse, and I knew it. "I'm sorry I didn't tell you."

Her tense shoulders dropped with defeat, and neither of us spoke for a moment. Then she wiped away her tears and stood up straight. This was one reason I admired her so much. She might cry to release her pain, but then she'd get right back up, standing even taller.

"I can't talk about this right now."

"I think we should, Elinor. There's too much happening, and I don't want this tension to remain between us. If we don't talk about it now, when will we?"

"I don't know, Will. Maybe whenever you had planned to tell me who you really were." She shook her head. "Hell, is Will even your name?"

My chest puffed up as I inhaled deeply. "It's William Hunter. Everyone calls me Will. My mother's the only one that calls me William. I don't remember my human name."

"How old are you?"

I gave her a small smile. "Very old." She didn't return the smile, and mine faded. "Centuries-old, Elinor. But my age doesn't matter. Even werewolves age slowly."

"Vampires don't age at all. So what happens down the road? One day I'll be all wrinkly, and you'll still look like this." She turned away as if realizing something. "I never even thought about that."

I stepped forward, and her eyes quickly changed to black when she looked up at me. "Don't think about that, Elinor. Okay? Listen to me. I don't care for you just because you're beautiful."

39

"It doesn't even matter." She shook her head. "Why speak of the future when we have none?"

I frowned at her words. "No one knows the future, except for maybe the Enchanteds among your kind and seers. We don't know what the future holds for us."

"We don't even know what we are," she argued. "What are we?"

Say it!

"You're mine." The defensiveness in her eyes faded, and I glimpsed a glimmer of hope before she quickly masked it. "And I'm yours. I've never felt this way about anyone before. I told you, I'll follow you anywhere, and I meant it."

I've proven that.

When she said nothing, I continued, "For a long time, I felt like it was better for me to stay away from others, to remain in my own world, apart from vampires and supernaturals. But you . . ."

"Stop!" She closed her eyes, shaking her head from side to side. "Stop, please."

"Why?" When I closed the distance between us, she grew tense. "Why? You asked me what we are, and so I'm telling you. I'm telling you what you mean to me." Then I reached up and brushed my knuckles against her cheek. For too long, we'd been beating around the bush about our feelings. I wanted her, and after this morning, I'd realized that I could lose her at any moment. "Do you not want to be mine?"

She swallowed and looked away, but I cupped her cheek and turned her head back to me. She was so stunning, her lips so plump, and I wanted to be reminded of her taste.

"Don't . . ." The word left her lips on a heavy breath, and I placed my forehead against hers.

"Tell me you want me, Elinor, because I know you do. I've had enough of this. I've had enough of only getting pieces of you in secret. Tell me you'll be mine."

"I can't."

She tried to look away again, but I wouldn't let her. "Yes, you can. All you need to do is say it."

"You're the son of the Vampire Queen, Will. That changes so many things."

I blinked rapidly and pulled away. "How different is that from you being the daughter of the Alpha? You're royalty among your own people, too."

"You know what the problem is. At first, I was just the Alpha-born, and you were a normal vampire. But you're not a normal vampire. You're a prince, and one that can walk in the sun."

I couldn't believe what I was hearing. I had never judged Elinor because of who she was. Her title didn't matter to me. She was doing exactly what I had feared she would—she was judging me based on my mother, my race, and the power I hadn't asked for.

The open door on the cage surrounding my heart slammed shut, and I stepped away from her. "Okay."

She looked at me, confused at my words. But I couldn't help her. The expression on her face had forcefully reminded me of why I had remained alone for so long. Why had I ever thought I would be accepted?

"Okay," I repeated.

The confusion on her face turned to anger. "I—I do want us, okay?" Her expression crumpled. "I do want you. But don't you see, Will? You and I can never be together. Never." Her voice cracked, and she looked away. I swallowed hard as she stepped around me, wiping at her tears with the back of her hand.

Her heart was breaking, but so was mine. I knew she was speaking the truth, I just didn't want to accept it. So this time, when she walked away, I didn't follow her.

5

ELINOR

I stormed towards Skye's room but took deep breaths to calm myself before entering. I pulled the door open gently and found Skye sitting up in bed, the wound on her head completely healed. Only a patch of hair was missing. Being werewolves, our hair proliferated quickly, so it would only take a few weeks before she looked like she did before.

My anger at Will faded as I plodded towards Skye's bed. She was staring down at her covered legs as if in a trance, her eyes unblinking.

"Skye," I said gently, and she looked up at me.

The moment our eyes met, I rocked back on my heels at the agony in her gaze. Skye had only ever had her mother. She'd never met her father and had been content with that. Only now, she was all alone in the world.

Her eyes began watering, and the dam holding back my own tears broke. I rushed forward and climbed onto the bed with her.

"She's gone, Elinor. She's gone!"

She was shaking her head wildly, and I grabbed her and

pulled her into my arms. We hugged each other as if someone was trying to pry us apart. She sobbed long and hard, the sound painful to hear, but I allowed her to cry. I let her pound her fists against my back. Finally, she lowered her head to my chest, and her sobs grew muffled. I didn't care that her nails were digging into my body as she held me close, and I pressed my face into her black curls, tears pouring from my eyes.

I felt utterly helpless to soothe her pain, and I hated it. She continued to cry in my arms, her firm hold on me not loosening, as if she was afraid I'd disappear if she released me.

"I'm here," I told her. "I'm with you."

I wanted to tell her I was so sorry for what happened. I wanted to tell her I'd avenge Ms. Clementine, but I kept those words to myself. Somehow, I didn't think that was the right thing to say just now. She'd been silent since she arrived, and I understood. Words wouldn't be enough. Nothing would ever be enough.

I couldn't imagine a world without my mother or my father and brother in it. I'd never imagined a world without her and Cyrus either.

I didn't want to. And thank the Goddess, I didn't have to. Sure, I was at risk of being shipped off to another pack, and Cyrus would have to return to the Demon Realm, but we wouldn't be pulled away from each other by the cold hands of death.

Still, I had a grim feeling that the world was about to get even darker. Whoever had been killing supernaturals and reanimating them wasn't doing it for the betterment of the world—that much I was sure of. What good could possibly come from so much death?

Skye finally pulled away, but we kept holding hands. I wiped at her tears with my free hand before wiping away my own. We sat for a moment in utter silence. Thanks to the spell Saleem had cast on the room, the noise from the world outside couldn't enter.

It was peaceful. And much needed.

"T-They made me watch," Skye stammered. So much for peace. Her head was bent, her eyes gazing down at her lap, and she squeezed my hand. "They tortured her to get me to tell them who had broken the cloaking spell they'd placed on me, who could possibly be powerful enough. They wanted to know who was coming after me. I was going to tell them, but my mother kept yelling at me not to. She said she could take it!"

We caused this! Oh Goddess, we killed Ms. Clementine!

The idea of Skye living with the horrific memory of her mother being tortured for the rest of her life filled me with intense sadness. And it was all my fault—mine and Cyrus's. Sure, Skye and Ms. Clementine were already in danger—at risk of being killed and resurrected—but we'd made things so much worse, forcing Ms. Clementine to suffer even more. If we had found them another way, maybe none of this would have happened, and Ms. Clementine would still be alive. But we'd had no other way of finding them.

"They wanted to know who'd broken the spell and said they'd let her go if I talked. I knew it must have been you guys, but I said nothing." She closed her eyes, and her face scrunched up. "T-They hurt her . . . so I had to tell them. But t-they—" She choked on her words, and I squeezed her hand to offer her my strength. "They killed her anyway."

She wasn't blaming us for her mother's death. I shouldn't blame myself either, I supposed, considering we were dealing with monsters. But just knowing that something I did cost Ms. Clementine her life was a heavy burden to bear.

"After a while, a man appeared through a portal. I'm not sure what he did, but some of the supernaturals were reanimated before he left. He released them, letting them kill the others left behind in the cells. I heard him talking to someone the whole time. He said they couldn't move everyone, so those too weak to receive the mark should be killed."

"Why did he speak so freely with you there? Who was he, do you know? Did you catch a scent?"

She swallowed hard. "I was on the floor bleeding profusely from my wound. I'm sure he didn't expect me to live, so it didn't matter to him what I heard. He didn't care that I was listening." She reached up and gently touched the patch of exposed scalp. "After the supernaturals in the cages were killed, I was left in the forest as bait. I never glimpsed the man who came through the portal, and he had no scent that I could make out."

She looked over at me, her eyes dull. "I wanted to die, Elinor. I-I can't believe she's gone . . . I begged them to kill me, too. What am I going to do without her? She was right in front of me. I could have—"

I hugged her, cutting her panicked words short.

I'm so sorry.

But sorry would not bring her mother back. All we could do was find a way to end this before the army of reanimated supernaturals grew too large.

Skye looked at me. "The one that you guys killed—did he have cat-like eyes and the arm of a werewolf?"

I shook my head. "No. He was a mash-up of different body parts together and had black eyes like a demon."

She shook her head. "He's not the one." Her eyes turned to black. "The one with the cat-like eyes? He's the one I'm going to kill."

I totally understood the way she was feeling. I'd felt the same way not too long ago. But I'd been angry at myself, furious that I'd been too weak to save her and Ms. Clementine. I hadn't been strong enough, and Skye had almost literally slipped out of my hand.

However, Skye had been forced to watch something that would leave her with a wound that might never fully heal. I knew, deep down, that I'd done all I could to save her the night they took her, and Skye had answered their questions, doing all she could to save her mother, not guessing that they'd kill her mother anyway.

"We'll find him," I told her, nodding my head once with finality.

Skye took a deep breath, not looking quite as defeated as she'd seemed when I first entered the room. If avenging her mother's death gave her a purpose and a reason to heal and get her strength back, I was all for it.

"Is it true that Will is here?"

I grew silent, my mind taking me back to the conversation Will and I had just had. Will had told me I was his, and he was mine. I'd been so happy to hear those words, but I couldn't move past the feeling that I didn't truly know the man standing before me.

He never should've kept something that important a secret from me. And Will had several chances to open up to me in the past. He'd taken me into that forest, he'd told me he'd never leave my side, he'd told me he cared about me . . .

But even if I'd known, how could I accept that he was the son of the Vampire Queen? And on top of that, he was a vampire who could safely walk in the sun? People finding out about his powers alone could start a war. And as it was right now, things were already a mess.

"Yes, he's here. He, um, followed me."

"Did he really? Can he truly walk in the sun? I overheard Cyrus telling Theanos that when he arrived."

I raked my teeth across my bottom lip. "Yeah. Without his

help, Cyrus and I probably would have died. So . . . I have him to thank for that."

Damn it.

Even though I was upset with him, I had to admit, I was very grateful he'd once again saved my life—and Cyrus's, too.

A few months ago, I wouldn't have been happy to have someone swoop in and save me. It would have felt like they'd thought I was too weak to defend myself. And weakness was something I never showed if I could avoid it. I'd never been one to hide from a fight, nor pretend I couldn't protect myself and others. But the situation Cyrus and I had been in was unlike anything I'd ever experienced before.

Without Will's help, we would have been goners.

Since leaving on this journey to rescue Skye, I'd realized just how many things I'd never experienced before. The dangers in this world were more significant than I'd ever imagined. That was the reason I'd wanted to leave the pack for so long. I'd wanted to see the world. I'd wanted to become a Guard to improve my raw strength and help others. In my pack, the best I could do as a female firstborn was become a Luna. But that wasn't enough for me.

A Luna was responsible only for her pack, and while that was honorable, I didn't want to be so restricted.

"You don't look too pleased that Will is here," Skye said.

I shook my head. At first, just the fact that he was a vampire had held me back. But the more time we spent together, the more I'd grown tired of my world and become more comfortable in his—more comfortable with him. So he was a vampire. So what? It was who he was as a man that meant everything to me. Sure, learning he could walk in the sun was a shocker, but it didn't change who he was as a person.

The thing I couldn't seem to move past, though, was that Will wasn't just an unusual vampire with charm. He was a

47

vampire with a title—a title that placed us worlds apart. I almost laughed aloud when I remembered thinking that we could be together if I went rogue. Now, even that wouldn't change anything.

"I don't know what to think now," I admitted. "I mean, was Will crazy to allow our friendship to get this far, knowing that discovery would make things impossible for both of us?" I palmed my face. "I fell for a bloody vampire prince."

"That says a lot," Skye murmured.

I looked at her with confusion. "What do you mean? What does it say? That he's a madman? I agree."

"He knew the risk and still pursued you. He followed you here and revealed his secret—a big secret. I don't think he'd do that for just anyone."

"I know that, and . . . I appreciate it. I just . . ." I closed my eyes as I exhaled. "I don't think we have a chance now. How could we? Sure, I could go rogue. But he can't walk away from being a prince." I shook my head as I opened my eyes. "At this point, I'd be willing to trade my life for a damn hut in the mountains, away from everyone and everything."

"You've considered going rogue, huh?" Skye didn't look shocked in the least.

"I've had enough of my father's selfishness, so I had planned on walking away from Elijah's proposal." I snorted. "Only he didn't even propose. He was being forced into our potential union, the same way I was. Still, I'm pretty sure I'll be leaving the pack, one way or the other. Too much has happened."

"I understand," Skye said, bending her knees and resting her head on the wall behind us. "I've decided to go with Cyrus when he leaves for the Demon Realm."

My chest tightened painfully at the thought of her leaving me. The idea of living without her in my life every day was like asking me which limb I wanted to lose. I didn't even want to think about it, though I couldn't say I blamed her for making that decision, especially now that her mother was gone. And if I had to leave the pack in order to live the kind of life I wanted to lead, Skye would've been left all alone. No, she was right to go with Cyrus when the time came.

Now that her mother was gone, there was nothing to stop her from being with Cyrus.

The world around us was moving too quickly. And on top of the challenges our normal lives threw our way, now we had power-boosted, mindless supernaturals to deal with.

"I think you should talk to him."

I glanced over at her. "Why?"

"As hot and cold as your relationship, or—" she cleared her throat, "—extra close friendship might be, he's making an effort. That's now very clear to see because honestly, I was skeptical. A vampire and a werewolf? Hilarious. But he's risked his own safety over and over again to be with you. Remember that. Besides, I'm sure you haven't told him absolutely everything about yourself, have you?" She pinned me with a pointed stare. "People have secrets. Cyrus has many, and while it's infuriating, I allow him to speak when he's ready and when he thinks I'm ready to hear. And you keep secrets from Cyrus and me all the time."

"Not major secrets," I grumbled.

"How long did it take for you to tell me you were sucking face with a vampire?"

"We weren't sucking face at that point," I said, a blush spreading across my face.

"Well, I know you wanted to, no matter how hard you tried to keep him at arm's length. But my point is, you keep secrets, too. And you're keeping him a secret from your father."

Damn. I'm in no position to judge anyone.

"You should talk to him. I think he deserves to be heard, especially after coming to your rescue yet again." Her eyes grew sad. "Don't wait. We can lose the people we care about in the blink of an eye."

I sank my teeth into my lip. Skye was right on all fronts. A part of me that had always tried not to need anyone was battling with the rest of me, the part that wanted Will in my life. What if I opened myself up to him . . . and he failed me? I'd already done that, in fact, imagining a life with him as a rogue wolf, free to be with whoever I wanted. Maybe that was why I felt so betrayed. His secret ruined that dream. Or at least, it looked that way right now.

I looked up at her again. "We spoke just before I came in to see you. He said that I'm his and he's mine, that he's tired of the way things are between us. Those were the words I really wanted to hear, but . . . the timing. I didn't know how to accept them."

"You're overthinking things. The problem is that you've never really been interested in guys. You didn't want—or need—anyone's protection. But a partner's purpose isn't only to protect you. It's to care for you, too. That's why Will wants to look after you. It's not because you're weak. It's because it hurts him to see you in trouble. I know Cyrus would move heaven and earth for me, and I love him for that."

"Okay . . ." I exhaled heavily through my mouth. "I'll try again. That is, if Will wants to talk to me now after I just rejected him."

"He will. Just don't lose the only man you've ever cared about because he's a little more special than you had expected."

Skye

*J*erked awake, a scream slipping from my lips, and Cyrus bolted out of the chair by my bed. I looked around the room frantically, but she wasn't there. My mother wasn't there.

It hadn't been just a dream, however. I fisted my pajama top above my heart as it threw itself against my rib cage. My mother's scream had been real. It was a memory that relentlessly echoed through my mind. I knew I'd be plagued with that memory, the horrible sound of her being tortured, for the rest of my life.

Cyrus pulled me into his arms. My eyes stung with tears and my breathing became labored as I clutched his shirt. Within seconds I was sobbing, the image of my mother's bloody face imprinted behind my eyes.

"It's okay, I'm here. You're with me." Cyrus ran his hands through my hair, offering me soothing words. "I'm so sorry I wasn't there to protect you. To protect you both. I'm so very sorry."

His words made my chest tighten, and the tears came faster. I turned my face into his chest, and the panic I felt slowly faded as I listened to his rapid heartbeat. He was hurting, too.

"Y-You did what you c-could," I said, hiccuping between sobs.

"I should have done . . ."

I moved away from him. "Don't. Don't say it. Nothing we say now can change anything. We'll never know what we could have done differently."

Goddess, my heart ached, and my body and my soul felt broken. But I also knew blaming ourselves would only make us feel worse. If Cyrus and Elinor took the blame for this, I would have to do the same. I had been right there but could not reach out to my mother as she took her last breath before they slit her throat.

I squeezed my eyes shut.

I wished I could be rid of the images in my mind, wished I could just reach in and pluck them out, but I couldn't. A part of me knew I needed to keep them. I needed to remember what had happened, so I'd have the strength to do what I had to do—kill that parasite.

And I would kill him—slowly and painfully. He'd murdered a piece of my soul, and I'd use that blackened piece to destroy him. His yellow eyes were branded into my memory, and that image was what I focused on. Not the memory of my mother's eyes slowly closing forever.

"Then I'll stop him." Cyrus's eyes were as red as I was sure mine were. "I'll find the one that did this. We'll find him. And we'll make him pay."

I was happy he'd said 'we.' I nodded, and he pulled me in for another hug. We stayed like that for a moment, and I soaked up the warmth of his body.

The world was a darker place than it had been before.

My mother's light was gone.

"We've got a location," Cyrus said. "We'll be going there shortly."

I sat up, wiping at a tear, and Cyrus moved a strand of hair away from my eyes. His gray eyes were heavy with grief, and we held onto each other's hands as if we'd both die if we pulled apart.

I squared my shoulders. "I want to go with you. I want to be the one who kills that mutant."

"I know. But we have to act now, and you're not well enough yet. But I promise you, if he's there, I'll bring him to you alive . . . well, semi-alive."

I smiled. "Okay."

I looked around the empty room, seeing only the chair by

my bed and a small table with jars of potions Saleem had used to help speed up my healing and replenish my strength. My smile withered like an old flower. I still felt fragile, and although I wasn't physically feeling pain, it felt like someone trapped my lungs inside a too-small box.

Each time I inhaled, the breath was a short one. Saleem had healed my physical wounds, but the emotional ones were getting worse. Would this tight feeling in my chest ever go away?

"I'm coming with you," I said. Beside me, Cyrus stiffened, so I clarified, "To the Demon Realm. I'll come with you."

"You don't have to decide on that now."

"I've made up my mind. When this is all over, I'll leave the pack and join you. Elinor will be leaving as well."

Cyrus frowned. "Do you mean she'll become a rogue? I didn't think she'd made up her mind about that."

I looked towards the door. "She will. I don't think she'll leave right away—not with all of this going on—but she will, for herself and for Will. Our world has always been too small for her. Her father's been pushing her too hard, confining her too much. I saw this coming a while ago."

"She loves him, although she hasn't fully admitted it to herself." Cyrus sounded so much like a concerned big brother, I smiled. He was always looking out for us both.

I nodded in agreement. "Will's risking a lot for her, too. He's not that different than you are, risking your family's wrath just to be here with us."

"I guess you're right," Cyrus mumbled, but from the look on his face, he wasn't pleased about being compared to Will.

Cyrus had always kept an eye on Elinor. After all, she was like a sister to him. And in his mind, he was only trying to protect her now. But unlike her father, at least Cyrus realized he couldn't stop her from living the life she wanted to live and loving who she wanted to love.

I yawned loudly, and he draped his arm over my shoulder and pulled me closer. We laid together in silence, and the sound of his steady heartbeat eased the tension that threatened to overwhelm me.

"I hope she knows what she's doing," Cyrus said. "It might not be so easy to walk away from the pack. Alpha Grayson will do everything in his power to stop her." I hummed my response, and Cyrus kissed the top of my head. "Go back to sleep. You need to rest more. I love you."

I didn't protest as my eyes began to shut at his command. "I love you, Cyrus."

Sleep claimed me once more, and this time, I dreamed of murdering the scum with the yellow eyes . . . then marrying the demon of my dreams.

6

ELINOR

I had to hand it to Skye—even in her vulnerable emotional state, she had dropped significant wisdom on me. Now I realized how much of an ass I'd been to Will. Not that he didn't deserve a little heat for keeping his background and his abilities a secret from me for so long. But I'd been so caught up in my own swirling emotions, I hadn't taken the time to consider how hard it must have been for him to reveal the secret at all. But he did . . . in order to save my life and the life of my friend.

It took a while to find him, but I eventually spied him on the balcony. I closed the door behind me soundlessly. Even though he must've known I was there, he didn't turn around.

I inhaled deeply, nervousness weighing heavily on me as I walked out and stood beside him. He didn't look at me, and I didn't look at him. We stood there in silence for a moment, scanning the numerous buildings before us. The night was a quiet one, except for the occasional scream in the distance.

"I was wrong," I said. From my peripheral vision, I saw him glance my way, and it gave me the courage to continue. "I . . . was in shock, and I didn't know what to think."

"It's okay," he murmured. "That wasn't exactly the way I wanted you to learn the truth about me."

"Still, I don't want you to think I'm ungrateful."

He turned to me, offering me a small smile. Goddess, he was such a beautiful man.

I looked into his blue eyes. "You saved my life again, and this time, it cost you."

He turned away to look out over the market again. "I'd do it again if needed."

Goddess, how can he be so sweet, yet so intimidating to me at the same time? How do those two things even go together?

He cared for me—I knew that. And now it was time I proved to him that I cared about him, too.

"I've been alive for a long time," he said. "I've seen horrible things, and I've done unforgivable things, Elinor. I won't pretend I haven't. I was feared and respected among my kind because I used my gifts to help vampires. If we'd met back then, you'd have thought me a monster. And I was one."

"Why are you telling me this?"

He turned towards me, his face half-hidden in the shadows. His eyes were red, and his fangs elongated. "You wish to know who I am, who I've been. So I'm telling you."

I swallowed hard. Will's vampire form had never scared me before, but I couldn't help the tingle of fear I felt as black veins began to crawl up his neck to his mouth. His skin turned pale, and his crimson eyes glowed, even in the shadows.

But my initial twinge of fear dissipated as my body moved forward to meet his lips without my conscious thought. His fangs grazed against my lips before they vanished, and he deepened our kiss. His lips were warm, not cold, and I sank into his arms as he gripped my waist.

Yes, I wanted to know about his past, his present, and his

hopes for the future. Maybe I should have allowed him to speak, but I hadn't been able to resist him. Vampires could be alluring, not unlike incubi and succubi. And Will had more allure than most.

Bleeders were ghastly, bloodlust-driven creatures, but Skins—vampires like Will—held a sort of charisma that pulled in their prey. Except for their scent, which could be picked up by other supernaturals, they were near perfect. To humans, vampires could appear almost angelic.

Our lips pulled apart slowly, and I reached up to trace the black lines on his chin. Even in this form, he was beautiful to me.

"That wasn't the reaction I was expecting." He sighed. "I also had a speech planned."

"Sorry," I chuckled. "I'm listening."

He kissed me quickly and pulled away, his eyes changing back to blue again. "I'm not the fiend I used to be, that I can assure you, but maybe one day you'll hear of the things I've done. I need you to know why I did them." He sighed. "I am in the unenviable position of being a vampire and a human. Unfortunately, neither species accepts me. So, many years ago, I terrorized the people of Earth because I was trying to prove to my kind that I was one of them, that I could be more ruthless than any other vampire. I was a legend."

"But I eventually grew tired of living like that. I stopped caring if my kind saw me as an equal. And for that, those who had once loved me turned on me and eventually ostracized me. It was a lonely life at first, wandering between both worlds, but I got used to it over time."

He looked away. "Life became very predictable. This is what leads many vampires to plague and terrorize other beings. They've lived for too long, and they grow bored with endless nights of death and sex."

"It sounds like torture."

"It is." He looked down at me and cupped my chin. "At least the killing part. Not the—"

"Yeah, I get it." The words left my lips in a rush, and Will chuckled at my embarrassment.

His eyes began to roam my face, as if he was looking for something. "Then, I met you. A little wolf who didn't scorn me or try to kill the vampire the moment she met me. That . . . was something that had never happened to me before."

"We're taught from an early age to either stay away from vampires or kill them. Only I didn't feel like doing either. There was no reason to." I smiled. "But I would have kicked your ass if you had attacked me."

His lips curved with a smirk. "I noticed that. It made me want to."

I frowned at that. "Y-You wanted to feed on me that first night, didn't you?"

"Yes," he answered bluntly. "For a while, I fought against the desire to taste you, telling myself I should leave you alone. But I couldn't. You were the first person to show me any semblance of acceptance in . . . well, forever. But I also couldn't feed on you, because I knew I wouldn't be able to stop."

I didn't know what to say to that. I should have expected as much. He was a vampire, after all. "Okay, so, what about your mother, the Queen?"

He shook his head and turned to face the door. "She eventually wants me to take her place, to be King. I suspect she's also waiting to see if I'm able to have children. She's forced human women on me in the past."

"Yeah, you can skip the gory details of your past sex life. But kids?" I made a face. "How can you have kids? You're a vampire."

"You're right. Most vampires are sterile . . . except for those with royal blood. My mother is the last royal alive, but for whatever reason, she's never been able to have a child the way her parents had her. So, when the time comes, she has to pass on her throne to a vampire she's created, a General."

"Oh," I spoke slowly with understanding. "So she's not your mother by birth. She's just the one that turned you." My eyes widened. "She thinks you can create a new race if you have kids, right?"

"Yes, a race of vampires who'll be able to walk in the sun. I still have everything a human does. It's not far-fetched that I might be able to impregnate a human or any other super-natural." He crossed his arms over his chest and leaned back against the balcony's railing. "Even so, she has said none of this to me. It's just a feeling I've had for some time. But I'm no longer an active General. I don't live at my mother's palace or among my kind."

I tapped a finger against my thigh thoughtfully. I didn't want to imagine a world with vampires who were capable of hunting night and day. We already had an issue on our hands.

"I've tried to stay away from them all." Will's voice grew dark with anger. "But my mother wants me to revert to being the vampire I used to be, and I was almost ready to give in to her demands. I've spent decades alone, Elinor. So, that's why I was . . . that's why I was in your little town."

"And now?" I asked hesitantly, and he turned to me, took me by the waist, and pulled me to him.

"I want nothing to do with the vampire throne."

"Would it be so bad?" I inquired.

He pinned me with a blank stare. "Yes. Yes, it would be. As the King of the vampires, I'd gain nothing but a kingdom of creatures who hate me. Yes, I'd have authority over them all, I'd rule, but that never enticed me. It still doesn't."

He looked up at the sky, and I found myself doing the same. "For a time, I lived almost like a king, ruling by my mother's side. At the time, having that level of ultimate power over others was intoxicating." He looked down at me. "But that kind of life can be restricting." He took a deep breath and continued, "What I want now is you, Elinor. And while I'll always be the Queen's son and have a connection to her, there are ways to hide from her, in this world or others."

He moved a strand of my hair behind my ear as the wind blew it across my face. "No matter how they hated me, I never had enough of a reason to truly be done with my kind —not until now, until I had you."

My swollen heart felt like it was going to burst out of my chest. "Do you mean that? You'd make that sacrifice for me?"

"Would it be any different from killing those Skins to protect you or revealing my secret to you? Tell me what else I need to do to prove to you that I love you, and I'll do it."

Did he . . . did he just say he loves me?

I waited to see if he'd looked shocked by his rushed words, but he only kept staring at me intently.

"Did you . . .? You just said you loved me, Will."

"I know," he answered as he reached out to pull me to his chest again. He placed his large hand over mine and squeezed gently. "I do love you, Elinor. For all the centuries I've walked this earth, I've never loved anyone the way I love you. I've never craved anyone like this. I've always thought I was better off alone."

He looked me up and down, and my stomach knotted at the uncensored emotion in his eyes.

"You, a werewolf and a pureblood, didn't care that I was a vampire. You accepted me." He shook his head as he laughed. "You kissed me just now because I showed you my vampire form. So, yes, my feelings are genuine, and I've had enough of not having all of you."

My heart melted and tears began to sting the back of my

eyes. I didn't know what to say. Will had broken through my walls so easily and chased away my fear of being vulnerable.

I looked down at my hands. All my life, my father had smothered me and made me feel that if I didn't have a mate by my side, I wouldn't be safe or protected. That was one reason I'd hated the thought of settling down so much. Until Will.

I looked up at him, my green eyes turning to black as I grew emotional. Will never belittled my strength, but he also never seemed to care that I was a firstborn female or worry about what was required of me.

He just felt honored that I cared about him.

He said I had accepted him, but he had accepted me as well. And it meant a lot.

"I love you," I breathed out, the words sounding a little foreign on my lips. "I do."

I exhaled as if I'd been holding my breath my entire life. Expressing my feelings and hearing him do the same had left me feeling weightless. I wasn't sure if this was what it was like to find one's mate, to feel loved, but I didn't care. Mate or not, I knew Will was telling the truth, and I knew what I felt for him was real, too.

I placed a finger against his lips as his head dipped to mine.

"I'm not going to marry Elijah."

"Of course not. You're mine now," he replied confidently. I rolled my eyes and my hand fell to his chest.

I could feel his heartbeat and the warmth from his body. "Okay, Slick, calm down. We have few things to take care of before you and I can go riding off into the sunset together, in case you haven't noticed. For one thing, we have to find the monster behind these reanimated supernaturals, along with the one who . . . murdered Ms. Clementine." I paused as I swallowed the lump that was growing in my throat.

His hands cupped my cheeks, and I closed my eyes. I could see Ms. Clementine's face in the darkness behind my lids, and my wolf stirred angrily. Will had only just confessed his feelings for me, so I decided to wait to tell him about my plans to leave the pack. For now, I'd just enjoy this moment with him.

I tipped my head back and gazed into his eyes. But the moment our lips touched, we pulled away as the sound of a commotion inside caught our attention. We looked at each other before moving at the same time.

What the hell is happening now?

Will

I couldn't remember my life before my mother turned me when I was twenty-eight years old. Even my memories from a decade ago were growing fuzzy, but I did know one thing for certain: the moment Elinor told me she loved me, I experienced a euphoria unlike any I'd ever felt before in my long life.

There was a time when I'd forced myself to be as soulless as other vampires. I'd strained myself to feel nothing but a thirst for blood. Now I couldn't help wondering what the hell I'd been thinking.

Elinor and I rushed back to the bar and found six Were-wolf Guards waiting for us. Cyrus and Theanos stood ready for a battle, their eyes black. The Guards had certainly taken their sweet time finding us, but I was curious to know how they'd even made it this far. The Werewolf Guard wasn't well-liked in the Black Souls Market. All I could guess was that they'd bribed someone into telling them if they'd seen Elinor and Cyrus.

A man with red wings was hard to miss.

Two out of the six Guards had transformed into their first form, each facing off with a demon brother. Their growls echoed through the bar, and Elinor rushed forward, stepping in front of Saleem and Scarlet.

"Enough!" she yelled. The wolves stopped growling immediately. "What are you doing here?"

"You need to come with us, Elinor," one of the Guards answered, his black eyes returning to blue. "Your father wants you to return home. We don't intend to leave without you."

"Are you giving me an order, Jonathon? Are you sure that's something you want to do?" Pride burned through my chest. Elinor definitely wasn't ordinary. "I'm not leaving, but you are. And you can tell my father that we found both Skye and information about what's going on."

Jonathon looked at the Guard by his side before turning to Elinor once more. "Elinor, we can't return without you."

"I'm afraid you're going to have to. But you can take Skye back with you," Cyrus said, stepping forward. "We've learned of another location where we might find other abducted supernaturals. We're heading there soon."

"You'll need our help. Then we can return to the pack together." Jonathon didn't look like he was going to take no for an answer. Maybe he wasn't aware of Elinor's stubbornness.

"I'm not going back home until this is done," she said, squaring her shoulders.

"We have our orders, Elinor. Don't make us force you."

Growls rolled through the bar like a wave, and animosity sizzled in the air as Elinor's claws appeared. I readied myself to act, my eyes followed the Guards' every move. I just prayed I wouldn't be forced to get involved.

Elinor turned to Cyrus and held up her hand. He stepped

back, as did Theanos, Saleem, and Scarlet. She growled low, but the sound was so deep, the dishes on the nearby tables shook with the vibration.

"I wouldn't force my hand if I were you, Jonathon."

Not heeding Elinor's warning, Jonathon charged at her. As I moved forward to help, Saleem placed her hand on my chest and shook her head. I clenched my jaw and exhaled as Elinor and Jonathon collided. In seconds, she had thrown him across the room, hitting multiple tables on the way. Then one of the transformed wolves also attacked Elinor . . . only to hit the ground hard when her fist connected with his face.

Elinor shifted into her second form, white fur bursting from her skin. She held her head back as a thundering howl exploded from her.

The Guards stood frozen, their eyes averted in respect. My hands fell to my side, and I fell for her just a little harder. After a moment, she began to shift back into her human form, and Jonathon slowly got to his feet, his eyes still averted.

"You'll return with Skye," Elinor told him. "She's healing, but she's still weak. It's not safe for her here. Ms. . . . Ms. Clementine was killed." Jonathon looked Elinor's way, regret morphing his features. "I'm not coming home until this is over."

"I'll take her." Theanos stepped forward. "I'll fly ahead with Skye. I can make it back here faster, and I can fill your father in on what's happened."

Jonathan combed his honey-blond hair back and stood up straight. He was utterly submissive to Elinor. "Okay."

She nodded and stepped aside, allowing the Guard to follow Cyrus and Theanos into the back to get Skye. Jonathon's eyes fell on me with surprise when he walked by, but he said nothing. I remained to the side, a silent onlooker as Elinor said goodbye to Skye. The poor girl was thin, but her eyes were bright and filled with something I knew all too well—a thirst for vengeance.

"Here." Saleem approached me and held out a small vile. "You'll need this."

We were alone now, except for Scarlet. Cyrus and Elinor had already gone outside to see the wolves and Theanos off. I narrowed my eyes at the old woman's cunning smile before taking the vial from her. I turned it over in my hand, its clear liquid shifting around inside it.

"This is a potion to mask my scent."

"You know your potions." Her smirk grew wider as her eyes narrowed. "I doubt there will ever be another like you."

I decided to ignore that comment. She was a black magic user, and it would be better for someone like me not to be on her radar. I pocketed the vial. "Thank you."

Then the door opened, and Elinor and Cyrus returned. Saleem took Elinor's hand in hers. "Elinor, I had no idea you were a white wolf."

"Well, yeah, I'm guessing you've heard the rumors. But it's not important."

Saleem's expression became grim. "I'm not so sure about that."

7

ELINOR

J combed my fingers through the grass beneath me and closed my eyes. The wind on my skin felt amazing, and I inhaled deeply, enjoying the crisp, clean air as animals called to each other in the forest behind me. That was when I realized I must be dreaming. I wasn't enjoying some solitude by the cliff back home. No, I was still in my room at Saleem's bar in the Black Souls Market.

Nevertheless, I decided to enjoy this moment of bliss.

Theanos had left with Skye a few hours ago, and Saleem had strongly suggested I get some rest. And I had definitely needed it.

Before me, the sea was calm, the waves small and gentle, and I lost myself in the soft sounds of them crashing against the cliff. I felt at peace, more than I had in a long time. My eyes opened as I tilted my head back to gaze up at the brightly colored sky. The picturesque sunset looked as if someone had splashed buckets of orange, red, and purple paint across it.

I sighed.

I wish the world was always this peaceful.

I knew death was a necessary part of living, but it could be painful and cruel. Skye was pretty tough, but losing her mom had left her reeling. I shook my head. None of them—Skye, her mother, or the other supernaturals we'd encountered—deserved what had happened to them.

I went over the information we'd gained from Arden in my mind repeatedly, but it offered no hints as to who was behind this mess. Considering that humans, werewolves, witches, and elves were all among the victims, it would be barbaric if someone from one of those species was behind what was happening. That, however, left thousands of other species to consider—dark creatures and otherwise.

I frowned. While we were fighting Arden, there'd been no humans there at all—only supernaturals with heightened abilities. So what were the humans used for? I pinched the bridge of my nose—speculating always gave me a headache. But for the life of me, I couldn't imagine the motivation of the person behind all this death. What was their goal?

Nothing in my eyes justified this kind of suffering. I didn't want to imagine the agony the supernaturals who were branded with that strange symbol had gone through. And the ones still missing would likely endure the same.

One thing I knew was that I wouldn't stop searching for the person responsible, and I knew Cyrus felt the same. Neither one of us would rest until the person behind Ms. Clementine's death—and the master themself—was found. Whatever Arden's master's plans were, I wouldn't just sit by and let them happen. I wasn't going to lose anyone else.

My lips twitched with a smile, and I brushed a finger against my lips as I thought of Will. My cheeks heated, and I chuckled to myself as I shook my head. Will was, indeed, an anomaly. I never thought I'd ever meet someone like him. I knew our future would be messy once I left my pack and he cut ties with his mother. But I was still looking forward to that life. So what did that make me?

Foolish maybe, but I loved him. I wanted the life I'd always dreamed of—with him.

Then my smile faltered. Could we have a family, though? Was it possible? After all the centuries he'd been alive, surely, he should have gotten someone pregnant by now—even accidentally. Having children always seemed like a distant priority before, but the possibility of having a child with Will made me realize just how much having a family really did matter to me.

I shook my head, needing to think of something else to calm myself.

The sound of grass crunching caught my attention, and I jumped to my feet and spun around. I relaxed when I saw Ione drifting towards me.

"Ione? Is everything okay?"

But when blood began to drip from her nostrils and her eyes turned black, I knew something terrible had happened.

"They . . . they know who you are. They're coming for the pack."

They? Who is . . . ? Oh, no!

I shook my head, my heartbeat spiking. "Ione, what are you talking about? Who knows who I am? Are you saying the pack is in danger?"

"Come back." She faded, becoming almost transparent, the trees behind her visible through her body, and I remembered I was dreaming. The world around us cracked and crumbled as blood rolled down her cheeks like tears. "Come back."

That was the last thing she said before I pulled myself out from the dream.

Bolting upright in bed, sweat soaking my clothes, I looked around the room frantically. I ran from the room towards

Saleem's office. The door opened as soon as I got there, revealing Cyrus, who was looking me up and down, no doubt having heard my frantic heartbeat.

"We have to go!"

"What's going on?" Will stepped past Cyrus to meet me. "Are you okay?"

"Ione mind-linked with me in a dream just now. She said they know who I am, and the pack is in danger."

"Shit," Cyrus hissed as his Adam's apple bobbed. "Saleem?"

"I heard," she called from within the office before appearing at the door. "I don't do portal spells, but I know a witch close by who does. Did this Ione give you a time frame?"

I shook my head, my heart still pounding. "No. She's a young Enchanted. All she could say was that they know who I am, and they're coming." I sighed as I closed my eyes and rubbed at my forehead. "They know who I am. Goddess, I sent them right to my pack."

"Saleem, please see if you can get that witch to create a portal for us," Cyrus asked, and Saleem nodded, then called Scarlet forward with a finger. Scarlet pulled her red hair into a high ponytail and checked a blade that was on her thigh.

"We'll be back shortly," Saleem said to us all before she nodded at Scarlet and they left.

First, our attempt to track Skye resulted in her mother's death when they tortured her about the cloaking spell, and now my pack was under attack because of me. I swallowed hard, my mouth going dry, and I turned away.

"This can't happen. It'll be my fault if anyone else dies." Someone touched my shoulder, but I moved away.

"Elinor, they could have found the pack through Skye or Ms. Clementine. Or even me. This isn't your fault," Cyrus said.

I turned to him. Although his words rang true, I couldn't shake the feeling of dread rising inside me. An image of my little brother bloody and dead on the ground appeared in my mind, and I swallowed hard.

Where the hell is Saleem with that witch?

"Hey—" Will held onto my shoulders to stop me from pacing. "Look at me. Cyrus is right. Losing control now won't do anyone any good. They found your pack. And no matter how that happened, we all need to act to protect your people."

"You can't come with us, Will."

His hands fell away from my shoulder. "You can't stop me, Elinor. If your pack is under attack, you're going to need all the help you can get."

"She's right." Cyrus nodded towards me, but his eyes were on Will. "The wolves might mistake you for an enemy during the battle. Because why would a vampire fight alongside wolves?"

Will seemed to think about that for a moment. "I haven't fed in a while, so I'll remain in my human form and my scent won't be as strong. And I'll have a beating heart. Besides, I'll be arriving with the two of you. They won't mistake me for the enemy."

"So that's it, then?" Cyrus narrowed his eyes. "When you don't feed, you slowly revert to being human. But when you feed, your vampirism returns."

"Yes, but I can only refrain from feeding for so long."

Well, that explains that.

"Okay, then. Come with us, but stay close. And be careful," I grumbled against my better judgment.

A portal opened within the office, and Saleem, Scarlet, and a young woman in her late twenties with a violet gem on her forehead appeared.

"This is Prudence," Saleem said, quickly introducing the

witch, and Prudence nodded to us all as the portal closed behind her.

"You're the Alpha child, yes?" She called me forward. "I'll use you to open a portal to your pack. Since we don't have the time to create a bottled portal, this is the quickest option. But it will drain you."

"I'll do it then," Cyrus offered, and I held my hand up.

My confidence had significantly slipped ever since the Guard trials. I'd let that tragedy make me forget who I was and what kind of strength coursed through my veins. Now, when something didn't happen the way I thought I should have, I doubted myself.

But no more. Cyrus and Will would accompany me back to the pack, but I was going to do this part alone, at least. I wasn't weak, and I would do it. My pack was depending on me.

I looked at Will, my love, and he nodded his head in encouragement.

"I can do it. I'll be fine."

"While you're gone, we can gather a party and check out the location we got from Arden." Scarlet's beautiful face was determined as she shared a look with Saleem. "We'll find you once we've learned more."

I nodded, silently sending her my thanks. Then Prudence began to chant, causing the gem on her forehead to shine as bright as her violet eyes. She held her right hand out before her, and a small swirling orb of energy appeared and steadily grew. I quickly realized the orb was pulling my power from me, but I withstood it, clenching my jaw and focusing on home.

The pack could be under attack at this very moment. The weakness I was feeling wasn't important if it helped us get there in time to help. Ione must have warned my father as well. But Theanos wouldn't have arrived yet to tell them

71

what we knew. If the pack was attacked before any of us arrived, they'd be completely unprepared for the horror that was about to hit them.

"Here." Saleem handed me a potion bottle. It was like the one she had given Cyrus, Theanos, and me to replenish our strength when we had first arrived and broken the cloaking spell shielding Skye. "Be careful, white wolf."

I took the vial from her as Cyrus and Will stepped into the portal. I gulped it down and closed my eyes as my body shivered and my energy swiftly returned.

"Thank you," I sighed as I opened my eyes. "We'll see each other again soon."

I nodded my thanks to Prudence and Scarlet before stepping into the portal, my eyes already changing to black as I called on my wolf.

Who knew what we were about to step into? I only hoped we weren't too late.

Elinor

The moment I stepped out of the portal, my heart plummeted. All around us, there was screaming. The thick smoke in the air had blackened out the sky, hiding the stars above. The portal closed behind me with a gust of wind, sending my hair flying wildly.

Cyrus shifted into his demon form, black mist rising from his body. His wings burst from his back and lifted him off the ground.

"We're too late," I whispered to myself.

An explosion erupted to the left of us, and Will's eyes turned red as his fangs elongated.

"We need to split up!" Cyrus called down to me, his eyes now as black as mine.

I started running, not sparing a second thought. "I'm going to the pack house!"

Will pulled up at my side, running effortlessly. "I'll come with you."

We rushed through the forest, and I shifted into my first form mid-run. I stumbled as my legs broke, then I ran on all fours as my hands turned into paws. I couldn't slow down. I needed to find my parents and my brother.

Ahead of us, a werewolf in its second form sporting a branded symbol threw a brown wolf from my pack into a tree. I howled aloud, my voice booming through the trees as I collided with the reanimated wolf before it could finish off the dazed brown wolf.

We tumbled to the ground together, but I hurried off, and Will took my place before the wolf could get up, ripping its throat out. Will caught up to me quickly, his right hand slick with blood. Our eyes met for a brief moment. The burning world around us slowed as my black eyes peered into his red ones. He smiled at me, flashing white fangs, and my wolf shook her head with a gentle growl.

Chaos was all around us, and I was on the verge of losing my mind with worry for my people, but with Will by my side, I couldn't help feeling a glimmer of hope that everything was going to be okay.

As I looked at Will now, his lips curving ever so slightly with a smile, my heart thudded like it never had before. We broke through the tree line at the pack house and skid to a halt. My home resembled a battlefield. I rapidly spotted my father's second form as he fought with a resurrected werewolf.

His massive brown claw swiped across the wolf's face as

his long tail slapped an elf that was approaching him from behind, the force of it sending her flying.

His eyes landed on me, and he howled as I did in greeting before his black orbs slid to Will by my side.

I looked at Will too, but at that moment, his eyes widened at something behind me. Then he abruptly grabbed me and threw me to the side. He blinked out of sight as I crashed to the ground and a lightning bolt struck the tree where I had been standing.

The witch's head lulled to the side, her violet eyes returning to pale green as blood sprayed from her opened neck. Her body hit the ground with a sickening thud, and behind her, Will inhaled deeply, black veins crawling up his neck to his cheeks and chin.

"Go," he said.

I growled low to tell him to be careful, then ran towards the house. I counted five resurrected supernaturals outside, but who knew how many more were scattered throughout the pack?

The moment I entered the building, my mother's battle cry met my ears. While in her human form, she sunk her claws into an elf's chest despite the rose vines wrapped around her body. The vines fell away, and she removed the elf's heart as the small thorn puncture wounds covering her body healed quickly. Our eyes met, but an explosion erupted in the kitchen, causing us both to duck.

Shit!

"Find Jackson!" my mother yelled. "He's upstairs! Get him and get out of here!" She ran off before I could argue, and I shifted into my human form.

I looked up the stairs and then in the direction she had run. I didn't want to run away. I wanted to stay and fight. However, Jackson was going to be the next Alpha, and keeping him safe was a priority.

Grinding my teeth, I ran up the stairs, checking each room and calling for my brother.

"Jackson!"

My bedroom door flew open, and Jackson ran out, his eyes teary and wide with panic. I scooped him up into my arms and held him close. His soft sobs had my chest tightening, and I gently placed him back onto the ground as his little body trembled.

"It's okay. I'll get you out of here, okay?"

"M-m-mother?" he sobbed. "F-father?"

"They'll be fine. But I need to make sure you will be, too. I'm going to shift now." Another explosion went off outside, and down the hall behind Jackson, I could see smoke rising to the sky through a window. "I need you to get on my back and hold on. Okay?"

"Elinor!" he screamed, and I spun around to find an elf with half of her face burned standing at the end of the hall.

"Jackson, I need you to run!"

He started shaking his head, and I picked him up and whisked him into the room as the elf came running towards us. "You can do this. You're going to be the next Alpha. I know you can do this!" He wiped at his tears, his heartbeat still pounding, but he stood up straighter. "Find a vampire named Will. Just yell his name the moment you step out of the house. He'll find you and take you to safety, okay?"

"But . . ." he said when the room door was thrown open.

The door flew off its hinges, and Jackson rolled to the side as I ran forward, slamming into the elf and pushing her out of the room. I needed to protect my brother at all costs, even if it meant dying in the process. We'd never been close, but he was still my baby brother, the one who would continue the Blackwood name.

Protect him, Goddess. Please, I beg you!

I listened as his little feet sprinted from the room, and my fangs elongated before I sunk them into the elf's neck. Her pained shriek exploded in my ear, then she gained strength I didn't think an elf could possess. She wrapped her arms around my body, squeezing tightly, trying to get me to release her. I held on even as one of my ribs broke, the pain surging through my body, and I wailed in agony. We continued to tussle, neither releasing the other.

Without realizing it, we both reached the open window, where the smell of burning flesh scorched my nostrils. I sank my claws into her side and pulled us both out the window. She didn't scream or even seem to care as the ground rushed up to meet us. I quickly reached up, snapped her neck, then pushed her away from me before tucking and rolling.

My shoulder dislocated as I hit the ground, and I groaned in pain.

Cries of suffering met my ears as I got to my feet. I froze where I was, staring at the pandemonium around me. More resurrected supernaturals had arrived, and my people were struggling. They were being slaughtered.

Goosebumps covered every inch of my flesh, and my breathing became labored. I spotted Will vanishing into the forest with a bundle on his back that I knew to be my brother. I sighed with relief, but tears slipped from my eyes as I saw a wolf I'd known my entire life—an elderly one who'd once read to me as a child—cut down by a bolt of witch lightning right in front of me. My eyes closed, misery settling on my chest.

"Goddess," I prayed. "Goddess, hear me, please. Save my people, I beg of you. I'll do anything, just save them. Please."

Thunder rumbled above, and my eyes snapped open.

Give me the strength to save them. Whatever the price, I'll gladly pay it. Please let me right this wrong.

The smoke above me cleared as a lightning bolt came rushing towards me. A chill went through my body as a slight breeze brushed against my cheek. Somehow, I knew I wasn't being attacked by a witch. This was something else. Something more.

I stood still, allowing the bolt to strike my body.

Very well, my child.

An eerily beautiful voice echoed in my mind just before the lightning bolt struck me, then another, and another after that. Burning hot pain rolled through my body, and almost unconsciously, I shifted, my bones breaking, my tendons stretching as I turned into my second form.

Smoke rose from the earth as more bolts struck the ground surrounding me. After a moment, I no longer felt like I was burning alive. Instead, the bursts of electricity were healing me, binding themselves to my body, strengthening me. Then, as abruptly as the lightning bolt barrage began, it stopped. All I could hear was silence . . . and the pained moans of my people.

I curled my fists, blinding power and rage filling me to the brim.

And when I opened my eyes, a growl strong enough to shake a mountain rocked my body.

8

CYRUS

*I*t wasn't black magic I was feeling. No, this was unlike any kind of magic I'd ever encountered. It felt old, crushing, and destructive. And it was rolling from Elinor in waves.

Lightning bolts had pummeled her, but she was still standing. For a moment, I'd thought a witch was responsible for the assault. But then she absorbed the bolts, and even the resurrected supernaturals stopped fighting, no doubt sensing a new power. I winced, blood rushing to my eyes as Elinor howled, her eyes and fur as white as snow.

Fear—that's what I felt as her cavernous mouth closed, and her large chest rose and fell rapidly. No one moved, no one breathed as electricity danced on her fingertips. This creature was no longer Elinor, but something else—something none of us could fight.

Roots erupted from the earth, the sound breaking the silence, and a reanimated wolf cried out as the vine wrapped around her body, crushing her. Elinor blinked out of sight, and my eyes widened.

She was fast, faster than even Will. Everyone started

looking for her, when she reappeared behind the elf that had summoned the roots. He spun around to face her, and her massive hand grabbed his face, covering it. Electricity engulfed the elf's body, burning him quickly, then Elinor threw him to the side like a used cloth.

The sky above us parted, and like before, lightning rained down on the earth, striking down all the resurrected supernaturals. Elinor continued her rampage, slaughtering with her hands as well as her newfound power. My victorious smile evaporated when I saw a Guard struck by lightning.

"No!" My wings flapped loudly. "Get to the house! Get to the pack house now! It's not Elinor!"

"Elinor!" Alpha Grayson yelled.

I hurried forward to stop him from approaching her. "It's not her! That's not Elinor!" Another Guard was struck by lightning. "We need to get out of here, now!"

Alpha Grayson howled, signaling for everyone to retreat. We grabbed as many of the injured as we could before rushing to the pack house. Because the god-like white wolf who'd once been my best friend was killing everything in sight.

Alpha Grayson grabbed Elinor's mother and pulled her to him as she struggled to go to her daughter. "She's okay," he soothed her, but he didn't sound sure.

I wasn't sure, either. Elinor had clearly been possessed. But by what?

I spotted Theanos's bright wings over the trees and took to the sky. He and Skye needed to stay away, or he'd fly right into this mess. I waved frantically, motioning him back, when a bolt of lightning struck my wing and sent me plummeting to the ground.

Someone yelled my name, but I wasn't sure who. The ringing in my ears was too loud. I could hear Elinor's footsteps, like a beating drum, as she slowly advanced on me.

Pulling myself up, I groaned and looked at my wing. A large chunk of my feathers had burned.

White eyes peered down at me as Elinor came to a stop before me. Behind her, many wolves were on the ground, and I prayed for Elinor's sake that none of them were dead.

She'd never forgive herself if they were.

"Elinor, it's me, it's Cyrus." My eyes turned red as I called on my magic. I didn't want to hurt her, but if someone didn't stop her, she'd do more damage than the supernaturals she'd just massacred. "Elinor, can you hear me?"

She bared her fangs, and saliva dripped from her mouth like raindrops. I winced as a thread of electricity shot from her finger and hit my knee.

"Elinor, it's me! It's Cyrus!"

Her white fur was stained red with blood, and I swallowed hard, trying not to make any sudden moves. I continued to channel my power into my hands. "Don't make me do this."

Her eyes darted towards my hands, as if she knew what I was doing, and I stiffened.

Her mouth closed slowly, but her chest rumbled with a growl. The moment she stepped forward, two gigantic swords formed in my hands, weapons that could bind her. Suddenly, a small voice echoed through the night.

"Elinor!" Jackson screamed as Will placed him on the ground.

"Jackson!" Alpha Grayson called, but the little boy was quick and got to my side within seconds.

"Sister, no!"

For the first time since she transformed, I saw an emotion other than rage in her eyes. She remembered. She stepped back from us, shaking her head wildly.

"Talk to her, Jackson. Help your sister."

"Elinor, please! Stop it!"

Her eyes changed back to black as the electricity running up and down her arms vanished. She staggered away from us and reached up to cover her face. She whimpered as if in pain, but when Jackson moved to go to her, I grabbed him. He was getting through to her now. But would it last?

"Elinor?" Will stepped forward, his hands up as he moved closer. "Elinor, remember who you are, who I am, who your brother is."

Her shoulder dislocated, and she fell to the ground. I could almost see her power leaving her body. Will caught her before she could fall, and the rest of the pack came running from the pack house.

Her shift was swift but painful, her cry burning itself into my mind. But Will held her close even as Alpha Grayson and Luna Clarice came to stand beside him.

He looked to be in agony, his face twisting as Elinor grabbed his hand. She squeezed it so hard I heard the bones break, the sound causing a few pack members to wince. When she returned to her human form, it was obvious that whatever had happened to her had taken its toll. Even her spelled Guard's uniform had been ruined, leaving her naked.

"Will," she breathed weakly before falling unconscious.

Elinor

*J*felt weightless as my body fell slowly. I didn't scream or thrash, just allowed myself to descend. It was as if there was no gravity, but I was sinking instead of lifting. Around me, everything was white. There was nothing to see but a vast white nothingness.

I didn't feel fear or anger, just profound peace and contentment. My thoughts were silent, and I sighed heavily.

As my body finally lowered to the ground, I closed my eyes, grateful for the chance to rest them.

I didn't feel warm or cold. I just was, and that was good enough for me.

Am I dead?

"No, child, you're not dead."

The unexpected voice seemed so familiar, yet I couldn't place it. Though I longed to rest my eyes longer, I opened them and sat up to discover who the voice belonged to. A female figure stood but a few steps away, wearing a white cloak that nearly camouflaged her in the pristine endless white of the environment.

I slowly started to feel more like myself as concern filled my thoughts. Who was she? The front of the woman's cloak was open, and her skin was as dark as the night sky. I got to my feet slowly, my heart now racing. She was wearing a white cloth lined with gold across her breasts, leaving her stomach bare, and a white skirt that became sheerer as it fell to her bare feet.

Stars were twinkling on her skin, and my eyes widened as a shooting star appeared at her right shoulder and darted down towards her left side.

She moved her cloak forward, shielding herself, and her face remained hidden. "I apologize. It's been a while since I've spoken to one of my children. I've forgotten my appearance is strange to you."

"Who are you?"

"Can't you tell?" Her voice was loud, thundering even, but oh-so-soft at the same time. "I have many names, but you call me Goddess."

I didn't know what to do with myself at that point. Should I bow or get on my knees? Unsure of the protocol when it came to addressing deities, I settled on placing my fist over my heart as I would with any other wolf and bowing to show my respect.

Her soft chuckle met my ears, and she walked forward. "You don't remember what happened, do you?"

I frowned at that, realizing that I couldn't remember what I had been doing or how I'd ended up here. I wasn't even sure where I was right now. Small portals appeared around us, showing bright moving images. I watched as I was struck by lightning. My blood chilled as I watched myself—or a wolf who looked like me—kill an elf. But when I saw myself standing over Cyrus with murder in my eyes, I had to turn away.

"No," I breathed out. "That's—I didn't want to hurt my own people."

"It was your first time using divinity. I'm not surprised you lost control. But I am pleased that you survived."

"I'm sorry, what?" I grimaced.

Can I even speak to the Goddess so informally?

"I mean, I don't understand," I said, trying this again. "What do you mean, Goddess? I-I wanted to save my people, not slaughter them."

"You asked for my help, child, and I gave it to you. None of your people died by your hand. Wounded, yes, but not killed. Steady yourself."

The portals vanished, but I could remember everything well enough now without them. I thought again of the intoxicated feeling I'd felt from the power I'd been given. I'd felt invincible . . . but even then, I'd known I wasn't the one in control. The power was.

I took deep breaths, trying to calm myself as the Goddess had commanded.

A few minutes later, I was able to say, "Forgive me. I don't mean to seem ungrateful. Thank you for hearing my prayer and answering." She nodded her head once, and I looked around us for a moment. "Where are we? You lent me your divinity, right? Was that how I could do what I did?"

Her head shook from side to side. "Where we are doesn't matter, and no, I didn't lend you my divinity. I awakened the divinity that was already inside you."

My face dropped with shock, and I rocked back on my heel. I took a large gulp of breath as I tried to make sense of her words. I didn't have any divinity. There was no way all that power was mine. "I don't understand."

"You're a white wolf, Elinor, one of my direct descendants. Why wouldn't you possess divinity? I understand the wolves among you who inherit my divinity are called Enchanteds, yes? If any of them were to transform, they'd look like you—a white wolf."

Well, that makes sense.

"You have small amounts of divinity, though more than other Enchanteds, which allows you to shift. You've proven yourself to be strong enough to have wielded this gift and survived." The Goddess stepped forward until we were face to face. "I will gradually lend you more of my power, in very, very small portions, to help you fight the coming war."

"At what price?"

Her cloak moved away, and she lifted her hand to my face but stopped short of touching me. I gazed at her hand, at the twinkling stars dotting her skin, and at the twirling symbol on her palm. The blissful feeling I'd experienced before returned, and my eyes closed of their own accord.

"A high one, my daughter. I'm afraid there will be a very high price to pay."

9

ELINOR

y eyes fluttered open, and I found myself in my room. I inhaled deeply, the sense of peace I'd felt at meeting the Goddess starting to fade. I wondered for a moment if that was what death felt like—endless serenity.

I caught my father's scent, and I turned my head to find him sitting by my bed. Neither of us said anything as we stared at each other. I smiled after a moment, and the worry in his eyes faded a little. He inhaled deeply, his broad chest rising and falling slowly. "How are you feeling?"

I nodded. "Good. How is everyone?"

"Everyone is fine, Elinor. You don't need to worry about anyone but yourself right now."

"Cyrus?"

He shook his head. "He's fine, all healed up. You've been asleep for a while."

"I don't think I was sleeping," I mumbled, and he frowned. "What do you mean?"

I folded my lips as I looked up at the ceiling. I wasn't sure if I should tell him—or anyone else, for that matter—that I had met the Goddess. Everyone was going to have questions about the beast I had become. My species wasn't fond of wolves who were different. It had taken years for the Enchanteds to be considered part of the pack, and even now, they still faced discrimination.

"What are they saying about me?"

"Never do that again."

I turned to look at him. His brows were knitted and dominance poured from him. His eyes turned black, and my body stiffened. But as fast as he grew angry, he calmed down.

His eyes became green again as he exhaled and pressed his fingers against the crease between his brows. He looked tired. No, exhausted. He just witnessed his pack on the verge of being massacred and then watched as his daughter turned into something that shouldn't have been possible.

"I'm sorry, Father." He looked up at me in surprise, and I reached a hand out to him. "I had to do it."

"I know that." He took my hand. It had been so long since my father and I had held hands, and even longer since we'd embraced each other. "But never leave like that without saying anything to anyone. Something terrible could have happened to you out there."

"Would you have let me go if I had told you?"

He shrugged, his tense shoulders relaxing a little. "I guess we'll never know."

"Oh, I think we know. You would have locked me in my room and had a witch spell the doors and windows."

He laughed lightly and released my hand. "I'm not that horrible, Elinor."

"Really?"

It felt nice to laugh with my father, but the fact that it had taken something like this to get us here, hurt. To everyone else, he was the Alpha, our leader and protector. But to me, he was the father I wished I was closer to.

The distance between us had just grown too wide over time. Even now, there were things I was struggling to forgive him for.

"There wasn't time to make a plan. Cyrus and I just reacted." I racked my teeth across my bottom lip and pushed myself up into a sitting position. "Ms. Clementine . . ."

"I know," he said, his voice low. "Theanos told me about it. That poor girl, seeing her mother die before her eyes . . ." He cleared his throat. "Skye is back at her house with Cyrus. As expected, Cyrus won't leave her side."

"Ms. Clementine deserves a wolf's burial, but we couldn't find her body."

"The Goddess will welcome her still."

I recalled the Goddess's odd skin and her sultry, eerie voice. Yes, the Goddess would welcome someone as loving as Ms. Clementine. I had no doubt of it.

I was still in shock that I had met the Goddess, and I was very grateful for her gift. Otherwise, many more of my packmates would have died . . . or been captured to suffer a worse fate. But what price would I have to pay in the end for the privilege?

"You know I never meant to hurt you, right? You're my baby girl. All I've ever wanted was to keep you safe and to make sure that when I'm not around, you're protected. But someone—okay, your mother—" he grumbled, and I laughed, "—pointed out to me that you're not only my daughter, you're the firstborn daughter of an Alpha. And that means you have the same strength I do. I'm sorry I haven't given you much credit for that."

I looked away, not knowing what to say. I hadn't exactly made things easy for him either, I knew.

Finally, I nodded, my words still failing me.

"I've said this before, but I feel I need to repeat it. I'm very sorry about what happened during the Guard examination process. And before you say anything, I'm talking about all of it—for using my influence to make sure you failed the exam and the way in which you failed. Levi shouldn't have tried to force you to kill Meeka."

"I still don't know why wolves had to die during that exam. It was barbaric."

"That's because it's never happened before. The examination is overseen with the help of witches, but we've recently found out that something went wrong. Really wrong." He looked towards the window, and I heard the voices of wolves outside drifting through it.

"One witch tasked with overseeing the exam had been experimented on, like the Arden creature you and Cyrus killed," he continued. "She removed the spell that would teleport any injured wolves out of the arena, preventing any deaths. Then she cast a trapping spell over the arena, forcing you all to fend for yourselves to the death. Eventually, she was found, but not soon enough. So many young wolves weren't meant to die."

"Goddess," I gasped. "Usually, the final examination isn't discussed afterward, so I didn't know what to expect. So only the families of those who had taken part in the exam would question what had happened, then?"

"Yes," he answered. "To make matters worse, The Council sensed something dark was brewing, so they had accepted more applicants than usual to increase our security forces. And they were right. Unfortunately, no Enchanted received a vision that might help us figure out what to do next. Nor have we learned any way to stop what's happening now."

It all makes sense now. Of course.

The Council had to have some idea of what was coming.

After all, they had Enchanteds working with them who would've had visions, prophesied darkness on the horizon for us. If only they'd foreseen what would happen in the arena.

"Now, at least, we know what's going on, thanks to you and the others. But you've been asleep for three days, and during that time, Council Member Levi arrived. And he wants answers."

My head whipped towards him, and my fists clenched tightly. Levi failed me in the Guard exam, despite what was happening, and he used a victim—my friend, Meeka—to do it. He was the last person I wanted to see right now. But news of what had happened during the attack on our pack would've traveled quickly. As the Council Member for North and South America, of course, he'd have crawled out from his cave to investigate.

"He won't take it easy on you, I'm afraid. And I won't be there to help you. I've spent too long trying to protect you, not that it did any good." He sighed as his eyes darted over my face with an admiration that struck a chord in my heart.

"You're on your own now. But you've done well on your own. You saved Skye and the pack." He scratched at his brow nervously, and it was both funny and uncomfortable to see my father, the Alpha, this unsettled. "I just want you to know . . . I'm proud of you. And I will call off your engagement with Elijah."

A face-splitting grin stretched across my face, and I jumped up from the bed and threw my hands over his shoulders. I'd had every intention of refusing to marry Elijah, but this was better. He placed his hand on the back of my head and held me close, and for a moment, we stayed like that.

Memories from my childhood of me never leaving his side surfaced in my mind. My chest ached as his hold on me tightened. Despite our constant fighting, I knew no one had my best interests at heart more than my father. Even though he had a shitty way of showing it sometimes.

"Even if we haven't always seen eye to eye, I realize you've always done what you thought was best for me," I whispered.

We pulled apart, and I exhaled, releasing all the anger towards him I'd held inside me. It was pointless, and now more than ever, we needed to be close. Now more than ever, I needed everyone I loved in my life to know I cared.

In this world, humans were the most fragile, but life could end at any moment for any species.

"Who is he? The vampire."

I turned and sat back down on my bed. I knew that question was going to pop up at some point.

"He's been lingering just outside the pack since you've been unconscious," my father said. "His scent is masked, but it's obvious he's a Skin. And even if he fought by our side the other night, Levi won't care if he sees him. So, who is he?"

"He's a good man, and someone we're going to need. But I can't tell you who he is, not yet."

He rubbed at his temple and nodded. "Okay. He protected Jackson and fought beside my pack, so I won't press the matter for now. But he's a vampire, Elinor. However you know him, I can't condone what appears to be a friendship between you two."

And there goes the truce . . .

"But—" He held a finger up. "I trust your judgment, and he did indeed save my son. For those reasons only, I'll turn a blind eye towards your relationship with him for now. Just keep this off the Council's radar, okay?"

"So, that's it? You aren't going to lose it? Or turn into the Big Bad Alpha and try to kill him? Who are you, and what have you done with my father? Wait, I get it . . . you're too afraid of my new powers to argue with me anymore. Wow, I never thought I'd see the day." I leaned forward, my eyes turning black. "Guess I'm the Alpha now, old man."

He rolled his eyes as he shook his head in exasperation. "Ha, ha, very funny."

I shrugged as I laughed. "I thought it was. But yes, I understand. And Will can be trusted."

He stood up and placed the chair against the wall, gazing thoughtfully at it before turning back to me. His eyes seemed to be searching mine for something.

"What they say about white wolves . . . That's what happened to you?"

I nodded, and he closed his eyes, as if he was praying to be wrong. "Levi's downstairs as we speak. Be careful what you say. You have more to worry about now than just these resurrected supernaturals. You'll be hunted, Elinor. There's never been someone like you among our kind. You know that, don't you? They will seek your power after for both good and bad reasons."

I swallowed hard but nodded.

"You can't trust anyone anymore, not even the Council," he continued. "You've always wanted to be known as more than just a firstborn female. Well, you've got your wish."

When he turned and left, I slid back down into bed. I didn't feel any sense of pride that I was more than just a first-born. In fact, a part of me wished that was all I was. But it was too late now.

More importantly, my father hadn't answered me when I'd asked what everyone was saying about me. Was it that bad?

Do they all see me as a monster?

I couldn't blame them. Watching myself in those portals had filled even me with fear.

I got out of bed and got dressed, burying my doubts deep within me. Right now, I needed to walk with my head held high. I had a horrible feeling about how this was all going to end for me. The Goddess had been surprised I'd used my divinity and survived.

But would I be as lucky if I had to use it again? Or would being more than just a firstborn cost me my life?

ELINOR

*I*t took an hour after my father left for me to gather enough courage to leave my room. I wasn't nervous about seeing Levi, but I was nervous about seeing everyone else.

In place of my hands, I saw paws drenched in blood. I could hear screams mixed with the sound of flesh sizzling as it burned, and I made a face as the horrific smell of it clogged my senses. Combing my hair and braiding it back, I tried to ground myself in the present. It was time. . . . I was as ready as I'd ever be.

There was no changing what had happened. There was no going back. No one from my pack had died as a result of my divinity being activated, and I needed to focus on that. Not only that, I had to find some way to make sure I remained in control next time. I clenched and unclenched my fists a few times to ground myself again before heading for the door. It was time to face Council Member Levi and everyone else who would have questions—questions I wasn't ready to answer. All I could say was, as a direct descendant of the Goddess, I had powers to help save my people. That was all there was to it.

No one had to know that my body felt different, as if it wasn't mine anymore. I'd always been able to feel my power, my strength within me, but what I was feeling now was different. It felt as if I was unbreakable now.

While getting dressed, I quickly noted the changes my body had undergone while I'd been unconscious. Others might not notice, but I realized I had changed physically.

My skin felt more sensitive than normal, as if my body was reacting to every shift in environmental stimuli. And my movements were more fluid and precise, while the muscles throughout my body were firmer, more defined. As I made my way downstairs, each step I took sounded louder than it should be, and I did my best to walk more softly.

Earlier, I had almost broken my window while trying to close it.

The closer I got to the staircase leading to the first floor, the more I could hear the voices of wolves inside the house. I realized my father was using the pack house to treat the injured. I wished I had known that before.

I swallowed hard. I wasn't sure I was ready to face the pack. Levi, I could handle. But I wasn't looking forward to facing the people I had hurt.

I got to the top of the staircase where I could easily see everyone lying on the ground below. Everyone grew silent, and all eyes turned to the stairs—and me. The house wasn't in as much chaos as I'd expected, but then again, three days had passed. Someone had even fixed the broken windows and doors already.

Nurse Hilary, who was bent over bandaging a wolf's right leg, stood up. She smiled wide, and my breath hitched as she placed her closed fist over her heart and bowed. I slowly descended the stairs, my heart hammering away inside my chest as everyone, even those on the ground, did the same.

Jackson came running towards me, and I picked him up as he threw his arms around my neck. My mother and father were standing on the left side of the room. Though teary-eyed, my mother also placed her hand over her heart and bowed with respect.

I swallowed again, trying to contain my emotions. I could see pride in my father's eyes as he, too, saluted me, and I held onto Jackson tighter.

"You saved us," a Guard who was helping Nurse Hilary said. "You saved all of us."

A chorus of whispers filled the room as everyone agreed. I placed Jackson on the ground, overwhelmed. Despite what I had done, my packmates were thanking me. No one was looking at me with horror.

"Thank you," I said, choking up with emotion. "I'm so sorry I hurt some of you. I truly am."

"Honestly, the scar left behind is interesting to look at," one man on the ground said with a laugh. He held his hand out to showcase multiple slightly inflamed lines running from his shoulder down to his fingers. The scar looked like lightning bolts were cascading down his arm, the same way they did from the sky.

Werewolves rarely scarred, since we healed so quickly. Only an extensive wound or an attack using magic scarred us. But, sure enough, each person on the ground with their injuries uncovered had scars.

I didn't know what to say, so I nodded. It wasn't as if I could say "you're welcome."

"Elinor, it's so good to see you again."

I turned around to find Levi standing behind me, his yellow eyes as hollow as ever. "I wish I could say the same."

The side of his mouth curved, and he threw a glance my father's way. "Still mouthy, I see."

"I doubt that'll be changing anytime soon."

My father cleared his throat, and I clenched my jaw. I gave Levi a thin smile as I interlocked my fingers in front of me. For my father, I'd show some respect. But I had no intention of pretending I liked this man when all I wanted to do was to punch him in the face. Something stirred within my chest as the tension in the room increased. Then a woman appeared behind him, her hair as white as snow.

Unlike Levi's smile, hers looked genuine. She placed her hand over her heart and bowed, and I did the same. "It's a pleasure to finally meet you, Elinor," she said, her prominent blue eyes twinkling with adoration. "I'm Faelen, an Enchanted."

Yup, the hair is a dead giveaway.

The name seemed familiar . . . and then suddenly, I remembered. The Enchanted my father had gone to meet just before Cyrus had killed the adracsas bounty hunter had been named Faelen. This must be her, but she was much more beautiful than I had imagined. Her face was straight, and thick blond brows hooded her eyes. There was an understated elegance to her movement, exactly as one might expect from the second-in-line to become the next Enchanted Grand Elder.

"It's nice to meet you," I answered. "Wait, where is Ione?"

I turned to Nurse Hilary, but it was Faelen who spoke. "She's doing well. I was just with her. She's a promising young Enchanted."

"Thank you." Hilary blushed with pride.

"If it wasn't for her, I wouldn't have known what was happening. She's getting stronger," I added, and Hilary smiled warmly.

Levi cleared his throat. "Elinor, I believe you and I have a few things to discuss."

I turned to Levi, and my father walked over to stand by my side. "We can all go to my office on the second floor."

Levi nodded. "Very well. I need to know everything that happened up until you arrived and how you came to have—" He looked me up and down. "—the power you used."

The corner of my left eye twitched. He looked at me as if I was a puzzle he was itching to solve, and my sense of unease grew. My wolf stirred inside me, and I inhaled deeply, trying to control it as he continued to speak.

"After that, a test will be done."

"A test?" I asked, my eyes lowering to slits.

I looked at my father, but Faelen moved forward, her hands facing upward. While I felt a deep sense of discomfort every time Levi opened his mouth, something about Faelen's presence and the way she spoke instantly calmed me. "From what Council Member Levi and I were told, you showed incredible power the other day. Combined with the fact that you're a white wolf, I think it's clear you are a descendant of the Goddess, like myself and Ione. But a simple divinity test will prove it beyond doubt."

"Okay," I answered and looked at my father once more.

He nodded reassuringly, and Jackson latched onto our mother's leg. I had yet to speak with her, but I saw in her eyes that she was dying to talk to me. And though I would have given anything to have been able to run to her, to have her tell me everything would be all right, right now, in front of Levi, I needed to appear in control.

I'd cry to my mother and allow her to curse me out for leaving later.

Elinor

"*T*hat's all you did?"

I nodded as Levi looked at me skeptically. "Yes, I prayed to the Goddess. That's all I did."

"So you're telling me that if I pray to the Goddess for power, I'll receive it?"

"It's highly unlikely since you're not one of her descendants." I hadn't meant for the words to sound rude, but they did, all the same. And I couldn't bring myself to care. "I assume my powers were awakened because of my divinity."

"So, in other words, wolves without divinity can forget about the Goddess ever hearing their prayers?"

"That's not what I said," I answered as calmly as possible.

On the outside, I appeared calm, but on the inside, I was seething. As I'd explained the things had happened from the night Skye was taken until the night of the attack, Levi had done his best to twist every word I said.

We sat in silence for a moment until he glanced over at Faelen, then added, "Well, your divinity hasn't been confirmed yet."

I was getting tired of this whole thing, and so, apparently, was my mother. "Are you saying that you think my daughter isn't a descendant of the Goddess?" she growled. "Do you think she got her power from something or someone else, then? And if it turns out that she doesn't have divinity, what will happen to her?"

My mother looked fierce, the way she always did whenever she defended Jackson or me. However, Levi didn't seem bothered as his yellow eyes fell on her. Nevertheless, she refused to back down and continued to hold his stare until he finally lowered his eyes.

"An alternative course of action will be taken—discreetly, of course. No harm would come to Elinor. But with the current state of things, Elinor being given power by anyone other than the Goddess is just one more problem we can't afford." He crossed his legs and took a sip of the water my mother had given him before he'd started this mockery of an interrogation.

"She'll join me to meet the other Council Members in Romania, and the test will be done there," he added.

He's kidding, right?

"I'm not going to Romania," I blurted out, and all eyes fell on me.

Levi's eyes narrowed. "It wasn't a request."

"With all due respect, Council Member Levi, I don't care. I'm not going to Romania."

His mouth turned downward with disapproval, but that didn't bother me in the least. There was no way I was going to Romania with this man. I could feel it, deep down, that he would do far more than just test for my divinity. For the Council and among many other species, women were viewed as somehow lesser.

The Enchanteds were a perfect example. Considering they were descendants of the Goddess and gifted with extraordinary powers, they should've been governing us all. Instead, they were under the Council's thumb just like the rest of us. Perhaps even more than the rest of us.

"Your daughter, an Alpha-born female and a firstborn, lacks discipline, Alpha Grayson. That won't stand. Our culture is built on respect."

The audacity of this man is staggering!

"Our culture should be built on respect that's mutual," my mother argued, and Levi snorted. "I don't approve of my daughter going to Romania, not with the threat we currently have knocking on our doors."

"You and I go way back, Alpha Grayson. This isn't the type of pack I thought you'd be leading."

"What exactly did you expect, Levi? Weak wolves without an opinion? I agree with my Luna and my daughter. I'm not sending my firstborn to Romania to be poked and prodded —ever."

I got to my feet at the same time my father did. He was an Alpha, and despite the fury in his eyes, he still had to respect the Council. But I didn't.

"My father is a great Alpha, and despite your petty remarks to the contrary, I think you already know that. And if you think women are not worthy of your respect, that they shouldn't have opinions of their own, you might as well just say so. But the way I see it, that's your problem. In the Blackmoon Pack, we stand by each other, males and females alike. That's how the Blackmoon Pack came to be one of the most respected, and that's why we'll stay that way."

I glared at Levi, hoping something would get through to him. But it was obvious he wasn't going to change. And he needed to know I wouldn't either. "A woman who was like a second mother to me was murdered. My best friend was almost killed and is now scarred for life. Members of my pack were murdered before my eyes. I'm not going anywhere. I need to stay here and help my people. If you insist on testing me, do it here. If that's not good enough for you, then too bad. My pack needs me, and I intend to be here for them."

"That's enough!" Levi roared as he got to his feet, his eyes changing to black as his voice thundered through the room.

My father quickly moved to my side, but despite the heavy weight of Levi's dominance, I had no trouble standing my ground. Then I took a step forward, and a surge of power exploded within me as I called on my wolf. Judging by the way Levi stiffened, I knew he could sense the power flooding from me, and he realized it wasn't something he wanted to tangle with.

"I won't be silent when it comes to my own life. I never have been, and I never will be. I'm not disrespectful—I'm just deciding my own fate. I'm not anybody's property, and I will have a say in what happens to me." I quickly glanced at my father, who was looking at me with something like pride, and took a deep breath. Then I turned back to Levi. "You're right, I'm an Alpha-born and a firstborn, and I was raised to be strong. A male wolf wouldn't allow himself to be treated like this, and I won't either. Just because I wear a dress, that doesn't make me less entitled to respect. But if it makes you feel better, I could put on a pair of pants, too."

I couldn't stop the onslaught of power pulsating inside me. My body temperature increased, and I could feel my dress growing damp under my arms. "I might not be a Were-wolf Guard, but I, along with two dark witches and two demons, was able to get information the Council couldn't during the months of keeping this threat a secret."

Levi's ears turned red. "And your pack was found because of your recklessness, don't you see that?" he argued. "Don't judge the Council's methods, child. You know nothing. Because you openly attacked them, they retaliated, and as a result, they attacked not just this pack, but also two others in their search for you."

That news hit my heart like a hammer, shattering it. I clenched my fists, my nails digging into my palm, and Levi smiled villainously. He knew he'd struck a nerve.

I didn't know what to do, what to say . . . so I simply let go. Both Levi and my father quickly stepped away from me as a lightning bolt flew from my right shoulder to strike the ground between Levi and me. I swallowed hard, a burning sensation blooming over my skin. I could feel electricity surging through my body.

I wouldn't listen to Levi. I wouldn't let him blame me for this. If he had done his job right, he would have found these people long ago. If he'd been smarter, none of this would have happened.

Still, his comment about me being responsible for the attacks on two other packs stung more than I cared to think about, and they threw my power and control off-balance.

"Elinor . . ." My mother walked towards me.

Faelen, who'd remained silent all this time, didn't move from her spot across the room . . . though the smallest hint of a smile was on her lips as she watched.

"Enough!"

My power vanished immediately as my father's growl shook the windows and doors. I hung my head as my chest rose and fell rapidly. I squeezed my eyes shut, my body still buzzing with power.

"That's enough," he repeated calmly. "Council Member Levi, Elinor is my daughter, and therefore, my responsibility. Fighting among ourselves now will solve nothing."

"She's out of control," Levi spat, and my father growled.

"Control can easily be learned. And there is no one more capable of doing it than Elinor. You see her as a potential threat, but she's the most powerful one here. Faelen, can the divinity test be done here?"

"Yes, Alpha Grayson," she answered.

I sat down, my legs growing weak.

"We will move the pack to a secret location. We don't know if they will attack again, and we can't risk that. We'll conduct the test before moving," my father said.

No one spoke as Levi sat down once more and the tension in the room subsided. "Fine, the test will be done here. But if Elinor loses control like that again, she's leaving with me. End of discussion. Yes, she's the most powerful one here, that's clear. But without control, she's a bigger threat than the resurrected supernaturals."

"I apologize for my outburst," I murmured, my eyes

downcast. I wasn't speaking to Levi, of course, but my father, and showing Levi that my father had control over his pack and his people in the process.

I'd overstepped just now, stepping in when my father was more than capable of defending himself and his honor.

"You may leave, Elinor."

I nodded at my father's words and got up without sparing a glance at Levi. I walked stiffly out of the room because I could feel the Council Member's yellow eyes on me. I had just challenged Levi, and I had a feeling he wouldn't let that slide.

ELINOR

*T*he sun's warmth on my skin soothed me on my walk through the forest, although the tingling sensation from the sweat pushing up through my pores felt slightly uncomfortable. Adjusting to the increase in sensation from my new power would take time. The wind combed through my hair gently, but I still felt on edge. Ever since the awakening of my new power, my chest ached. It felt like the power was pooling there, waiting to be released.

I wanted to release it, but who knew what would happen if I did? What I needed right now was a distraction and some space away from that yellow-eyed weasel. I growled as I twisted my dress, the tight corset squeezing me. I missed the freedom I felt when I wore my Guard's uniform, and oddly enough, I missed the adventure Cyrus and I had embarked on to save Skye and . . .

My thoughts trailed off as I thought of Ms. Clementine—and how badly everything had gone. The world was in shambles, and I didn't want that. But I realized deep down that it was the adrenaline rush I'd ached for all these years.

I'd ached to be out in the world, but now it was bittersweet.

I frowned.

Okay, it was now mostly bitter.

I had seen so much death. And I felt like I was going to overload with the memory of it. I'd always known the world could be a dark place, but I hadn't really experienced it for myself until now. Yet the things I'd witnessed hadn't made me want to turn and run. No, they made me even more determined to protect those who couldn't defend themselves.

I gazed down at my hands and then folded them into fists. Now I had more power, power that could do so much, but Levi wanted to lock me away.

Desperate to release the excess anger I felt every time my thoughts turned to Levi, I pulled my dress up at the sides and started to run. As trees passed me by in a blur, I laughed, thrilled by the significant increase in my speed. At this rate, I had to be faster than even Will. The power in my chest warmed my body as it flowed to my legs, pushing me even faster. Soon the bright forest grew a little dark, and I realized I was deep in the woods, where the thick canopy of trees above obscured all but a few rays of sunlight. Here, no birds were singing, and at night, it was the most dangerous part of the forest. This was where Will had saved me for the first time.

This was where everything began for us.

That night, he'd killed two of his own to save me, a young and foolish wolf who'd ventured out on a full moon. Blinded by rage at my father's attitude and actions, I hadn't exercised even a modicum of caution on a night where I was most vulnerable. Knowing I couldn't shift because of the full moon hadn't stopped me from running off, angry at the world.

I smiled as I thought of the way Will had appeared, cloaked in darkness, and then had followed me until I was back on my territory. We'd come a long way since that night. I thought of the way he fought by my side the other day, even at the risk of his own life.

I felt relieved that he seemed to have gained my father's respect. It was nice to think that maybe the man I loved and my father could get along. But I knew my father's lenience with this situation would only last until I told him I'd be leaving to become a rogue, a bounty hunter.

As I strolled forward, all I could hear was the sound of insects. And in my mind, it was as if the insects were saying the things I knew my father would. He'd argue that I had fallen under some kind of trick, that my feelings for Will weren't real.

I snorted.

He'll want to see Will's head on a spike.

"Why are you always wandering off?"

I spun around, and Will removed the large hood that was covering his face. I ran to him and threw my arms over his shoulders. I hadn't realized how deeply I'd missed his voice until I heard him speak. His arms held me tight at my waist as he spun me around. If I hadn't been as strong as I was, he would have snapped me in two.

Finally, my feet touched the ground once more, but he didn't release me. Burying his nose into my neck and hair, he inhaled deeply, and my body liquefied.

"Stop sniffing me like that. It's disturbing."

He chuckled. "Come on, it can't be that bad."

I pulled away from him as a thought occurred to me. "You can't be here. I mean, we're not on my territory right now. But still, you can't be this close or out during the daytime. What if someone sees you?"

He pointed to his cheeks, which weren't the standard pale white of a vampire. That meant he hadn't fed yet. "All they'll see is an ashen man. And I mask my scent when I walk during the day. That potion Saleem gave me was the strongest I've ever had."

I scoffed as I shook my head. "Looks like Saleem just gained herself another customer." Then I remembered what she and Scarlet had said they were going to do. "I wonder how things went with them. They said they were going to check out the location Arden had given us."

Will shrugged. "I don't know. I haven't heard anything. But there is something I should tell you." I wasn't sure I wanted to know, judging by the seriousness in his voice. "I'm going home."

I knew I hadn't wanted to know. "I may or may not be going deaf. Please, tell me you didn't just say you're going home?"

He turned his back to me, the tail of his cloak brushing against his boots. "My circumstances have changed, so I need to return. But I won't be gone for long." He turned to face me. "I'm also going home to check if my mother knows anything about what's happening."

"You suspect her?"

"I wouldn't put it past her. But whether or not she's involved, I need to discover if she knows anything."

I really didn't like the idea of him going home. "She won't find it odd that you care?"

"I won't give her that impression. If she's involved in anything that might affect our kind positively or negatively, as a General, I need to know about it."

I nodded, despite the ache in my chest. "I understand. How long will you be gone?"

"I'm not sure. Long enough to not seem suspicious, but I won't be gone forever." He walked back over to me and cupped my cheek. There was something about his tenderness that always made me relinquish my trust to him. "Are you going to miss me?"

I looked up at him and nodded. I breathed deeply as his thumb caressed my cheek, and my eyes fluttered when he lowered his head to mine. My arms slid around his waist as his lips claimed mine passionately.

"I was so worried about you," he mumbled against my lips. "There was nothing I could do, and I couldn't get too close. It was maddening."

"I'm sorry," I whispered back. "I was unconscious."

For some reason, it didn't feel right telling him about seeing the Goddess. But I'd wonder why, later.

He squeezed, tightened his hug, then ended our kiss. "What happened to you? You seem different, somehow. Even your body has changed."'

I smirked. "I wasn't aware you were such an authority on my body."

He arched a brow, obviously surprised by my flirting, and his eyes flashed red. "I'm not as much of an authority as I'd like to be. Maybe I should get a closer look, just to be sure." He smirked, and his blue eyes twinkled in a way that made my toes curl.

"But seriously, what happened?"

"Have you ever heard the stories about white wolves? About them being descendants of the first wolf, a direct descendant of the Goddess?" He nodded. "Well . . . those stories are true. Like Enchanteds, I have divinity. But while Enchanteds cannot shift, white wolves don't lose that ability."

"'So, you're the strongest among your kind?"

I made a face. "I-I don't want to say I'm the strongest. There are probably other white wolves out there some-where, and they might have even more divinity in them than I do. But I'm the only one I know of who has had her divinity powers activated. Even then, it's not like I'm unbeatable."

"After what I saw the other night, the power you wielded,

Elinor, would pose a challenge even to my mother. But you must learn to control it."

I turned away from him, as Levi's words came back to me. "I wounded so many of my pack that night. And I was the reason my pack and two others were attacked in the first place." I bit down on my lip. "Maybe Levi was right."

Will rested his hands on my shoulders. "I don't know who this Levi fellow is, Elinor, but your pack would have been attacked eventually. Until we catch whoever is behind it all, no one is safe." He turned me around to face him. "Thanks to you, Skye, and Cyrus, we now have an idea of what's coming. Focus on that and the lives of the wolves you saved that night —nothing else."

He pulled me into a hug, and we remained like that for a moment. He was right—the attack was inevitable. The Council clearly planned to continue hiding information in its misguided attempt to protect everyone. And while keeping secrets would prevent a mass panic, a random attack—especially on a full moon—would leave countless dead. Nobody would be prepared.

It was just hard for me to forget what the Goddess had shown me. I still couldn't shake the memory of the fear of me in everyone's eyes, even Cyrus's.

Cyrus.

I needed to go see both him and Skye. "I spoke to my father about you."

Will pulled away, but his hands lingered on my waist. "And what did you tell him?"

"Nothing much. I only told him you're someone he can trust, someone who can help us in the war that's coming. He appreciated the fact that you saved Jackson, and said he'd turn a blind eye to you being a vampire—for now."

"Hmm, I don't think my mother will be as understanding if she finds out what's happening between us."

"I'm sure my father's lenience will only last until I tell him I'm leaving the pack. At least he said he'd call off everything with Elijah, so I'm saved from having to do that myself."

"I'm sure he won't approve of you and me, but he might surprise you and support you. You never know."

I shrugged as I moved his cloak over his shoulder. He was wearing a black cotton shirt with the sleeves pushed to his elbows, and black pants tucked neatly into his boots. I touched the exposed skin on his arms gently, enjoying their warmth.

"We'll see," I grumbled. "You being a General is going to make things way more difficult for us."

"Yes, it will. But I can handle my mother."

I looked up at him. "Are you sure about that?"

"Yes, but I won't be a General for much longer. I've had enough. So, I'll follow your example and do what a little wolf has more courage than me to do."

"How? How will you just walk away from being her successor? I think you said it yourself, Will—she's not going to let you go so easily. Especially if you can father children and potentially create a new race."

"Royals don't die often, so they only rule for several centuries before passing the throne onto the next royal in line. It's nearing the time for her to do that, so she must pass the throne on to someone, even if it's not me."

I nodded. "I see. It's almost the same with werewolves. My father will step down as Alpha after Jackson comes of age."

"Exactly," he confirmed. "As for escaping her, I know of ways to make it so she can't find me. I just haven't felt the need to use them until now. Just leave my mother to me, and I'll let you know if I discover anything useful."

Elinor

I glanced over at Skye, and she gave me a small smile. I swallowed hard and nervously returned it, then looked down at the symbol Faelen had drawn on my stomach. This divinity test made me anxious, but I was doing my best to hold it together.

I was lying on the ground naked, with a white cloth over my breasts and hips. The symbol on my stomach was a circle with words I wasn't familiar with written in the center. Faelen drew it with a concoction of herbs she had prepared that, oddly enough, smelled like lavender.

"Relax," Faelen said from across the room as she blended other ingredients in a small wooden mortar bowl. "Inhale the lavender. It'll calm your nerves."

As lovely as the lavender smelled, I couldn't forget where I was and what I was doing.

On my left sat Levi and my father, and on my right were my mother and Skye. Ione was present as well, watching closely as Faelen worked, obviously trying to absorb as much knowledge as she could. Meanwhile, I was lying in the center of the room, surrounded by lit candles. I felt like a sacrificial lamb.

The divinity test was a longer process than I'd thought it would be, and the longer it stretched on, the more nervous I grew. However, I was thankful that Faelen was performing it here, where I was surrounded by people I knew and trusted. Except for Levi, of course.

Faelen suddenly groaned, and when I looked at her, I saw her staring out at nothing, her eyes white. She rocked back and forth on her heels for a minute, then her eyes returned to their regular blue, and she looked around the room as if trying to remember where she was.

She took a deep breath. "I was just informed that two more packs were attacked."

I sat up, grabbing the cloth over my breasts so I'd remain covered. "When?"

"Who contacted you?" Levi questioned.

"A fellow Enchanted. She's a member of one of the packs under siege. That makes five packs that have been ambushed."

My father exhaled audibly. "Once we finish this, I'll have Connor follow up with those other packs."

I lowered myself back to the ground and listened as Ione questioned Faelen about how she could mind-link with someone while conscious. Ione told her that so far, she'd only been able to do it via dreams, and even then, it was hard. After a brief explanation and a promise to go more in-depth with her later, Faelen gave the girl a small hug, then entered the circle and stooped down beside me.

She placed her hand under my head and helped me into a semi-sitting position. "Drink."

She placed the wooden mortar to my lips while muttering incoherent words under her breath, and I closed my eyes and drank the foul-smelling potion. It was surprisingly warm as it slipped down my throat, and she lowered my head back down to the ground. My body felt weak almost immediately, and as much as I tried, I couldn't move.

I could hear Faelen muttering more words, but they sounded more and more distant. With my eyes half open, I watched as she straddled me, drank the rest of the potion, and then began rubbing her hands together.

I focused on the sounds being created as she rubbed her hands together, and then my body jerked upwards as she pressed both hands down on my stomach. The next instant, I landed with a loud oomph inside my room. Faelen watched me silently by the door as I stood up and looked around in confusion.

"Uh, what just happened? Did we teleport or something?"

"No, we're inside your mind, Elinor. You designed this room, probably for comfort."

"Okay," I drawled. "So, did you do it? Do you know if I have divinity?"

She chuckled as she walked towards me. "I did, and you do. But that was something I already knew." She strolled over to my dresser and picked up a small hairbrush I'd used as a baby. "You realize Levi feels threatened by you, don't you? You were smart to refuse to be taken to Romania."

"Why?"

She turned to face me. "I'm sure you've already sensed his intentions. He'd do anything to get the power you have. He's tried and failed in the past to gain the kind of power given to Enchanteds. That's why his eyes are yellow. One of his experiments went wrong."

"Why?" I asked again. "Why does he want more power?"

She shrugged. "To become the head of the Council, or maybe to declare himself the king over all werewolves? Who knows? But he's definitely power-hungry. That is why I arranged to meet you here and speak with you. I wanted to warn you to watch your back."

"But why should I trust you? You work for him."

Her face twisted with hate. "I don't work for Levi or the Council. The Enchanteds serve the Goddess, and even though some think less of us, we do what we can to help and protect our species. We're werewolves, just as much as those who can shift."

"I know that. And I think it's wrong to treat Enchanteds differently simply because you can't shift. I've been thankful to Ione more times than I can count for all the ways she's helped our pack. I don't know what we would've done

113

without her." I walked over to her. "But I think there's another reason you're doing this. Am I right?"

"You saw her, didn't you?"

I tried not to react, but she was inside my head. If she'd wanted to, she could've searched through my memories to get the information she needed. I should have been happy she had asked.

"Yes."

"And will there be a price to pay for wielding the power you have?"

"Yes, but I don't know what."

She nodded. "That's fine. I just wanted to make sure that if Levi ever discovered a way to take an Enchanted's power, or yours, he'd suffer for it."

I wasn't sure what had occurred between Faelen and Levi, but she was definitely out for blood. "What did he do to you?"

"Not me, personally," she answered. "But a friend of mine, an Enchanted, died during one of his secret experiments. The Council did nothing about it, simply swept it under the rug. I'm just waiting for the day he slips up, and I get to kill him myself."

I said nothing in response, because really, what was there to say? If Levi had been performing experiments on Enchanteds, he should have been removed from the Council and charged long ago. My guess was that the rest of the Council was as curious as he was.

Still, now that I had this information, I knew my instincts were right. He was scum and deserved to be treated that way.

"Are you ready to go back now?" she asked.

"Okay," I answered, and the room around us fell away.

I woke up with a loud gasp and saw Faelen on her hands and knees, panting beside me. She was glowing with pale blue light, and looking down at myself, I noticed I was, too. It was the same blue I'd turned when I touched the weeping willow in the Dragon Territory.

"Does she have divinity?" When Faelen nodded, Levi stepped forward, waved his hand, and the candles went out. "Good. The pack's evacuation can now begin. But the entire pack can't be moved at all at once if you want the location to remain secure. It will have to be done quietly and over a week's time."

He turned to me. "Elinor?" My chest was still rising and falling rapidly as I slipped on a robe my mother had ready for me. "You'll be going to a separate location."

I refrained from looking at Faelen, but I'd never forget her warnings about his obsession with power, nor the information about his secret experiments on Enchanteds.

"No." My mother stepped forward. "Elinor needs to stay with us. Why do you want her to go to a separate location? The test proved she has divinity. She can learn to control her powers as easily with us as she can anywhere else."

"Easily" was a stretch, but I remained quiet. Levi didn't look like he would budge on this, and I wasn't going to object to going. No doubt he'd suggest he be at the same location with me . . . and that would allow me to take him down should he try anything.

If I had to be the bait, so be it. The Council had been created to protect our kind, not experiment on and kill us for their benefit.

"This isn't up for debate. Elinor's safety is now a top priority. She'll be hunted from all sides when this gets out. If she falls into the enemy's hands, we're going to have more trouble than we can handle."

My mother made a sound of annoyance at the back of her throat and turned to my father, but he made no move to object. Then she looked at me, and I held my hand out to her.

"If I'm going to practice controlling this new power I've

gained, I can't do that around the pack, especially while we're in hiding. It's okay, Mother. I'll be fine. I promise."

"If I may?" Skye interrupted. "I'd like to accompany Elinor. I've been studying to become a pack doctor. If I'm there, I'll be able to help Elinor if she injures herself." Levi looked contemplative for a minute and then nodded.

Suddenly, a portal appeared in the room. My father acted immediately, positioning himself in front of my mother, Skye, and me. Levi only turned to face the portal, his eyes turning black to prepare for a fight, and I couldn't help wondering how skilled he actually was.

A foot appeared from the portal, and my father's warning growl was loud and bone-chilling. When I saw the person who stepped out, I rushed out from behind my father, Skye by my side.

"Saleem!"

Scarlet was carrying the old woman in her arms and both of them were covered in blood. Their clothes were almost shredded, and they looked as if they had been attacked by an animal.

Scarlet staggered, then fell to her knees. "Help her."

ELINOR

"It's okay, Father. I know them!"

Scarlet lowered Saleem to the ground, and Faelen and Skye immediately began to check her wounds.

"You need help as well," I told Scarlet, but her teary eyes were on Saleem, now lying on the ground, her heartbeat faint.

"I'm fine. Just please, save her."

"Who are these people?" Levi asked.

"They helped us find Skye," I answered without looking his way.

I knew that if anything happened to Saleem, Cyrus would spiral. First, he'd lost Ms. Clementine, and now it looked like Saleem might not make it.

"Grayson, she needs help. Let's take her to Nurse Hilary. She'll know what to do," my mother suggested. My father nodded, then carefully lifted the wounded witch.

Saleem was unconscious, and blood gushed from a deep wound on her head. I prayed to the Goddess that she'd be alright. I watched them leave, nodding at Skye before she ran off with them. And that left me alone with my mother . . . and Levi.

"So now there are witches and more demons in wolf territory," Levi said, and I turned to stare at him, licking my lips.

I couldn't believe he'd actually said that, not now, not when we faced such a grave threat. But I decided not to call him on it. I was starting to realize that Levi's self-directed purpose in life was to get a rise out of everyone. So I turned and walked away, my mother by my side.

"You may remain here if you wish, Council Member Levi," my mother called over her shoulder. "Our cook will prepare anything you want. My husband will return shortly, and you can discuss your departure with him."

"Of course, Luna Clarice. And Elinor's departure as well."

My mother growled as we finally exited the room. "I've never wanted to rip a man's throat out as much as I do right now."

"Wow, Mother, I'm impressed. He can hear you, you know."

"I don't care," she said, and I grinned. "As for you, I haven't forgiven you yet for leaving. And for avoiding me since you've come back."

My smile fell away as we hurried through the house and then took the path outside leading to Nurse Hilary's place. "I haven't been avoiding you, truly." I sighed. "But I knew you and Father would have stopped me from leaving, and I had to go."

"I know," she mumbled. "Did your father speak to you about Elijah?"

"He did. But honestly, I would've called off everything myself, if he hadn't."

"You've changed." Her voice was low and filled with a sadness that stopped me in my tracks. "I'm not sure what you saw out there, but it was nothing good. I can see it in your eyes. You were always eager to see the world. But whatever you saw out there made you grow up a lot in a short amount of time."

I looked down, at a loss for words.

She chuckled. "Sadly, you're also even more outspoken."

I couldn't help laughing at that, and she took my hand into hers. She gazed at me with so much love tangled up tightly with sadness that neither of us said anything. My eyes burned, and I hung my head and inhaled deeply to stop the tears from forming.

"After the tragic events of the Guard exam, your spunk seemed to disappear. I was getting really worried. But you're back now, and I'm proud of you. You've always stood up for yourself, and now you can stand up for others, too."

I wiped at my eyes. "Thanks, Mother, for everything. I love you."

She kissed the palm of my hand, and we continued on our way to Hilary's. Bolstered by my mother's love, I made a vow to myself. I wouldn't let my fire go out again. No matter what happened.

Elinor

Scarlet took a sip of her tea and continued her story. "Saleem and I had gathered about fifteen others—witches and demons alike—and we went to the location Arden told us about. There, we found over thirty supernaturals, already branded and resurrected."

"Goddess," Skye murmured under her breath as she looked at Cyrus.

She looked a little more like herself now, thank the

Goddess. Her eyes weren't as sunken and the patch of hair she'd lost was growing back faster as well. Both she and Cyrus had been locked away in her house while she healed, and he didn't look nearly as pale now. Obviously, they'd been helping each other.

Cyrus hunched forward, his elbows on his knees, as he listened to Scarlet speak. My father, Skye, and Faelen had stayed while Hilary treated Saleem, and Levi had come later. With Skye and Faelen's assistance, Hilary had treated Saleem's wounds and was now applying her bandages. Witches were fast healers, but not as fast as werewolves. It would take some time for the older woman to recover . . . but she would, thank the Goddess. Only after Saleem was treated did Scarlet allow Skye to tend to her wounds. As a succubus, Scarlet would heal up in no time.

"What happened?" Cyrus asked, and Scarlet shook her head.

"We were outnumbered, but of course, we anticipated that. We had planned our assault carefully, and we were ready for greater numbers. But we didn't stand a chance when the real danger showed himself—a vampire General."

My eyes widened, and Cyrus and I looked at each other. "A vampire General?"

Although Scarlet knew what that meant to me, she kept it to herself in front of Levi. "Yes. He massacred the others. Saleem and I barely got away. She made a portal to the bar, but when we got there, more reanimated supernaturals were already waiting for us." She closed her eyes and leaned forward. "I've lived at that bar for years. It's all gone now."

"I'm sorry for what happened to you," Levi said, his words clipped. "But this vampire General . . . Did you see him? Was he branded like the other supernaturals?"

"He was commanding them."

Though I tried, I couldn't swallow the lump that had

formed in my throat. Vampires . . . Vampires were behind this, after all. I smoothed my brows out with a finger and dropped my gaze to avoid anyone catching sight of the confusion and panic within it. No, Will couldn't be involved. I wouldn't allow myself to even think that. But . . . he was heading home to see his mother. What if she already knew of his involvement, of his relationship with me?

"How would vampires be able to resurrect other supernaturals? They don't have that power, do they?" I asked, looking for any other answer.

"Remember what Saleem said, Elinor? Anyone can access and wield black magic." Cyrus reclined in his chair, a grim expression on his face.

I knew what he was thinking. He was wondering if Will had been playing us.

"But we can't go after the Vampire Queen just yet," I said.

"The hell we can't!" Scarlet yelled. "One of her Generals killed fifteen people."

"And more will die if we act without proper planning," Cyrus added. "Even if every werewolf pack came together, as well as all the witches, we still wouldn't be strong enough to wage war on the Vampire Queen. We'll need allies, other supernaturals."

"We'll also need more proof that the Queen behind this," my father added. "A General may have been there, but we can't storm Vampire Territory with only that information. We have very little information on vampires to begin with. Who knows what they're truly capable of? Walking in blind is a good way to get a lot of people killed, Scarlet."

"The General had some kind of unusual ability," she mumbled. "Before they were killed, a few demons and witches were caught in some kind of spell, frozen where they stood, screaming as if they were being murdered."

"There are rumors of some vampires possessing abilities,

yes." Levi touched his chin thoughtfully, and I caught Skye staring at me. "With that factor to consider, we definitely can't act blindly. We have to get eyes inside the Queen's castle. But that won't be easy."

"What if we could get a spy inside, and we confirmed the Queen was behind all of this? What then?" I asked Levi, though I was looking at my father.

He knew I was speaking about my friend. I wasn't going to tell Levi about Will—ever. I already knew how he would react. He would only accuse Will of being involved, of being sent out by the Queen to gain our trust—my trust.

"If this spy could provide useful information on the vampires, their defenses and abilities . . . We'd be able to end the vampire race, once and for all."

"We don't have the time to get a spy, not when two more packs were just attacked," Cyrus said. "They are targeting wolves because werewolves are a vampire's greatest threat, their natural rival. The more wolves they kill or abduct, the less there will be to fight against them when the time comes."

Cyrus has a point.

"And after what Elinor did, they'll definitely want to take out the werewolves first," my father added. "We need to hurry. And we should start by getting the other species on board, letting them know what's coming for them. If we don't come together and present a united front, they'll pick us off one by one."

"I'll head back to Romania and notify the rest of the Council," Levi said. "Faelen, you can remain behind. That way I'll be able to easily relay any messages I might have. Alpha Grayson, I trust you'll reach out to other packs in the meantime, telling them to prepare themselves for an attack. Women and children unable to fight should all be sent to secure locations."

"We'll do that," my father confirmed.

Levi turned to me. "Elinor, you will still have to be moved."

"Yeah, I didn't think that was going to change," I answered absentmindedly.

A clap of thunder rumbled outside, and I sank in my chair.

William.

Will

There were no birds, no animals, no life. The land was vast but dead, and the creatures that had lived here had polluted the earth with their deaths over the years. Vampire Territory was nothing but death and darkness. The skies were blackened out continuously by clouds with the help of my mother's dark witches. Anyone turned by the Queen was guaranteed to gain an ability, but from time to time, a witch, a fae, or any other supernatural who had magic that was strong enough, would usually retain some of their magic when turned.

That was how my mother now had three Enchanted Seers who kept her updated on world events. Thanks to a spell I hired a dark witch to perform for me a few centuries ago, I was shielded from her Seer's eyes.

Other vampires who retained their abilities were accepted and integrated into vampire society without question. Yet because my abilities were radically different than any other vampire and included walking in the sun, I was treated as an outcast, even by those who had also retained some of their abilities. The hypocrisy of it all hadn't escaped me.

Up ahead, between several black rotten trees, stood my

mother's castle, a dark, looming structure designed to strike fear into anyone that saw it.

Bleeders—the mindless vampires I detested so much— lingered in the forest outside the castle. They'd followed me from a discreet distance for the last two hours, probably out of curiosity. I left my carriage five miles back because the starving beasts would've only attacked and eaten my orthros, my two-headed wild dog. The small towns that once occupied the land had been wiped out centuries ago. Whenever food was delivered to the castle, the bodies were then given to the Bleeders.

Rarely would a Skin like myself eat their prey. Newborns unable to control their hunger were more likely to do that, but Bleeders ate everything—skin, flesh, and bones. Sometimes they even attacked each other, feasting on the weak among them.

With my cloak removed, the castle guards could see me approaching, and they opened the looming steel gates. The castle was quiet except for the sound of soft chatter that died when I entered the court. Only vampires from my mother's Council and their covens lived within the castle itself, along with all the guards and Bleeders. Scattered across the land were other covens that lived separately, like those who chose to be closer to humans.

I ignored the whispers that drifted to me, murmurs from newly turned vampires who had only heard of me and those who hadn't seen me in a while. But I wasn't bothered by any of it as I made my way through the castle. The less time I spent here, the better.

The halls were dark and depressing, the walls covered with paintings of the royal family and elders long past. There was a time when I'd walked these halls with the swagger of a king, drunk with the power I had, the respect and fear I commanded. Now, this place felt like a prison.

Sometimes the hunger inside me missed the savagery, the screams of the dying, and the taste of blood tainted with fear. But because all things release chemicals—depending on their moods—I'd found a prey's blood tainted with ecstasy or bliss was a thousand times better than fear. To me, at least.

"Will, you're back."

I stopped in my tracks and turned to face the vampire who spoke. A woman, a past lover I detested, was grinning at me with her pet fae walking on all fours beside her. The small fae woman was plump and clearly well-fed, but she was also only food.

She clung to Levia's side, both out of fear that other vampires would kill her if she was separated from her master and out of sick, twisted devotion. There was a time when I had a pet, multiple pets even. But now, even the thought sickened me.

"Levia, how are you?"

She stepped forward and placed a hand on my chest. "I've missed you, Will. Why do you insist on living elsewhere? You're a General. You belong here."

"No thanks to you. Now, remove your hand."

She smirked and flicked her brown curls over her shoulder, flashing her pale neck. "Don't be like that, Will. What happened between us is in the past. I never meant to betray—"

I grabbed a chunk of her hair, and my eyes changed to red.

A deep crease of pain emerged between her brows. "Wi—"

"Say my name again, and I'll rip your throat out."

Her mouth clamped shut, and her pet by her feet whimpered. I inhaled the scent of her fear, and the beast I tried to keep in chains stirred inside me. I pushed her away, and she fell to the ground, hatred filling her eyes. She'd sided with most of the Council during a petition to have me removed as a General. I'd never forgive her for that.

Of course, my mother's word was law. So when the Queen killed the vampire who'd started the petition and warned the others against ever doing it again, the matter had been put to rest. In a way, they'd done me favor—at least now I knew who my enemies were.

I continued on my way, leaving her and the other vampires staring behind me. After making it to the sixth floor of the castle with no one else stopping me, I stood outside my mother's chamber. My scent had returned, but she wouldn't have been curious about why I had masked it. Vampires often masked their scent to blend into crowds when outside of Vampire Territory.

I pushed the door open and walked in.

The double doors to my right were open, leading out to a large balcony. I could see my mother's shadowy silhouette behind sheer white curtains where a vampire servant helped her to dress.

"My son," my mother drawled happily.

"So, the prodigal son returns."

I looked to the left, where my brother Cain lounged on a chair, his blond hair pooling in his lap. We stared at each other unblinkingly, neither of us saying anything more. I felt his power flare as he tried to pry into my mind, searching for my greatest fear so he could use it against me. I arched a brow, a clear indication that I knew what he was doing and that he was wasting his time. I had mentally prepared myself before coming here—not only to face my mother but also my brother and his ability.

He smirked, and his power died away.

Cain was one of many who'd wanted me removed as a General. That hadn't surprised me—he'd never bothered to hide his hatred of me. My mother had declared that I was to be the next King, but as the older brother, he felt he was entitled to the crown first. He not only hated me for the title I didn't want, he coveted the powers I possessed. And that made him hate me even more.

"Hello, Mother," I answered as she stepped out from behind the curtain.

She was wearing a black mesh dress, its tight sleeves covering her arms to her wrist and hanging off her shoulder. The dress contrasted with her milky skin and left nothing to the imagination. I cast my gaze downward, both out of respect to her and because only her long black hair was covering her bosom.

"I missed you." She came to a stop in front of me, and I held my head up. "But why are you here? You didn't send word you'd be returning. How are things at Vivian's coven?"

Her eyes were a dazzling ruby red, the color covering the white of her eyes to reveal her true nature. As beautiful as she was, she was also clearly a predator.

I got straight to the point. "I'm here to speak to you about what is going on outside of Vivian's coven. Supernaturals are being abducted and branded with a symbol that leaves them compliant to somebody's wishes. And they're much more powerful."

"So?"

"Are you involved, my Queen?"

Cain stood up. "This is nothing you need to concern yourself with, brother."

"I'm not speaking to you, Cain. But I'm a General. If you two are involved in this, I have a right to know."

Cain laughed loudly, but it was dry and without humor. Our mother turned away, no doubt sensing an argument on the horizon.

"You haven't been a General in a long time." Cain stepped forward, and I sucked in a breath, causing my teeth to graze the inner flesh of my mouth. "You don't care about the covens or our species. You wander around, living among those lesser supernaturals, living among our food. You care even less about being our mother's successor, yet still you walk in here and demand answers. Know your place, brother."

I wasn't interested in arguing with Cain. I was here to speak with my mother, not him. But, of course, he would be present. The Queen was rarely seen without him by her side. Yet she didn't want him to be King. I wondered how much that stung him.

"That hasn't changed the fact that I will be King, brother. I am a General, and if something is happening that affects our species, I need to know about it. End of discussion."

Cain took another step forward, his fangs descending. "You don't deserve the throne. You never have. I've been here by our mother's side, while all you've done . . . "

I stepped forward, dismissing Cain by turning my attention to our mother. She waved her hand at her maid, and the female bowed and hurried from the room.

"Are you behind all the supernatural disappearances?" I asked her. Behind me, Cain hissed, but I continued to ignore him. "If you are, Mother, I need to know about it. I'm the one who is out among them. I can uncover far more information than whatever you've been given."

She sauntered to the open balcony doors. "For centuries, they have forced us into this lonely little corner of the world. It's time for us to occupy the land my father and forefathers once did."

I tried not to react, but my fists clenched nonetheless. Vampires, by their nature, caused many deaths, but this was taking it too far. This scheme stunk of Cain. I knew that much for sure.

True, centuries ago, some lands now occupied by supernaturals were considered part of Vampire Territory. But that was before I was born and before Amythia was Queen. From the stories I'd heard, things were very different back then. Vampires mixed with society. Vampire Territory flourished with life. The kings and queens ruled differently than my mother did. Amythia allowed Bleeders and Skins alike to run amok . . . and the land showed it.

"They—" She pointed outside. "—didn't stop until we were forced permanently into a corner. There are animals who have more freedom than we do, William. You know it's true, and that needs to change. We can't walk during the day, but we won't need to. Don't you understand? The supernaturals we take will help us regain what is ours."

"Why was this kept from me?"

She turned to face me, clasping her hands behind her back. "I sent you to that town for one purpose. That is all you need to concern yourself with!" She began pacing the room, then stopped in front of me again. "You're to be my successor. I'm doing what I must to expand your domain. That is all you need to know."

I shook my head. This wasn't what I wanted to hear. I hated that Elinor's pack had been attacked and couldn't help feeling as if it was somehow my fault. "Mother—"

"Enough!" She held her hand up, cutting my words off. She was my mother, but she was also the Queen. She could still kill me in seconds if she wanted to. "You got the answers you came here for, didn't you? Why are you pestering me about this, William? I know you've changed—I can see it— but I thought this would make you happy."

I thought of Elinor, of her courage, of her determination to live her life on her own terms. For too long, I'd been the Queen's puppet. But no more. "Cain can have the throne, and I'll remain a General. I don't wish to be King."

"Ungrateful," Cain hissed. "My Queen, I told you he

would not see the beauty in our plan to reclaim what's rightfully ours."

"Why should I be grateful to inherit a place that'll be destroyed because you're starting a war? Why should I be grateful for lands that will be empty of supernaturals and humans—or our food, as you call them—because this ridiculous plan you came up with turned them all into mindless things, and those left will fight to the death? You didn't think this plan through, Cain." My eyes remained on the Queen as I spoke to Cain, and I knew they turned to red as I grew upset. I wasn't going to let Cain or my mother pin this on me. "Vampires have been pushed into a corner for decades. We've been behaving the way we're expected to. Why were we not pariahs back then as we are now, Mother?"

I could feel Cain's eyes burning into the back of my neck. "How fucking dare you!" he shouted.

"Leave," my mother said to him, her lips barely parting. But the command was explicit. "Leave!"

I could almost hear Cain grinding his teeth on his way out. The second the door closed, her hand came down hard on my cheek, the slap echoing through the room. I staggered backward, blood immediately rushing into my mouth as I adjusted my broken jaw. Her long pointy nails had sliced my skin as well, and I held my jaw until the skin healed enough to stop the bleeding.

"I never again want to hear you speak like that, William. I forbid it. That attitude is the reason you've lost favor among our kind."

"But did I lie?"

Her jaws clenched visibly, and she paled. When her white skin turned gray, I knew I was pushing her to the limit. "You've forgotten what it was like when you stood by my side, as Cain is now. Things were better then, so much better." She reached out, as if to touch the cheek that she had just slapped but stopped herself. "Have you truly forgotten what it was like?"

I hadn't. And that was why I had no desire to recreate that world. My days of being her lap dog were over. I wasn't fooled by this journey down memory lane or her reasoning for doing this horrible thing.

One thing still wasn't clear, though. I frowned. If this was Cain's initial plan—and I was sure it was—I didn't put it past him to be planning something else, too.

Reclaiming land that had been lost couldn't be the only purpose behind targeting all these supernaturals.

She waved her hand, dismissing me as she turned away. "Focus on your duty in preparation to take my throne, and allow Cain and me to do what we must. If I hear you complain about this again, I'll have your head. Do you understand?"

I turned to leave the room. "Yes, my Queen."

"And William?"

I paused without turning to face her.

"No matter how far you run, you'll always be my son— and once the worst among us. You contributed to the way we're perceived, remember that."

13

ELINOR

yrus, Skye, and I had been sitting in a comfortable silence for the past fifteen minutes as a candle burned beside a small painting of Ms. Clementine. Cyrus had gifted it to her on one of her birthdays. He had done one for Skye and me as well.

Because there'd been no body, a proper werewolf burial could not be done, so this would have to do. Skye was sitting between me and Cyrus, which allowed us both to hold her hands. She'd stopped crying a few moments ago, and now a peaceful silence filled the house.

"The Goddess has her now." I squeezed Skye's hand, and she nodded, but her bloodshot eyes remained on the painting.

Beside her, Cyrus was looking at the floor, his fist clenched so tight, the knuckles were white. I knew he was trying to contain his need to act against the Vampire Queen. But all we had to go on right now was the fact that Scarlet and Saleem had encountered a General. I hated to say it, but Levi was right. We couldn't move forward without confirmation that the Queen was behind it all.

I hadn't said anything, but I was hoping Will could confirm her involvement, or if she was, in fact, the master villain.

As for myself, I felt depressed because things had just taken a turn I wished they hadn't. I was growing more and more eager for Will's return, to see that he was safe and to confirm what he'd learned. I was forcing myself to not think negatively, but it was giving me a headache.

Theanos had left to go home, carrying news of what was transpiring to the Dragon King. He doubted they would target the Dragon Territories—vampires were simply no match for dragons. Still, it was best to make them aware of what was happening.

In the meantime, Cyrus planned to work alongside the Werewolf Guards. The following day, he would leave us to visit the last two packs that had been attacked. Darian would go with him.

"Supernaturals weren't the only ones taken. Humans were taken, too. But we haven't seen a human that's somehow been changed," Skye grumbled as she sniffled loudly. "Don't you guys find that weird?"

"Or maybe we just haven't run into any newborn vampires yet," Cyrus added. "The supernaturals can attack during the day, and the vampires can do the rest at night. I'm sure that's what their plan is. Humans don't have any magic to be enhanced. But if they've been turned, they're more useful."

Skye inhaled deeply and then blew out the candle. We all stood up and placed our fists over our hearts before bowing to the painting. "Why are they doing this now, though? That's the question."

"Will didn't know," I blurted out, and Skye and Cyrus looked my way. "He didn't."

"You don't know that, Elinor," Cyrus said. When I shook my

133

head, he continued. "Why did he come here? Did he tell you? Did he ever tell you what brought him to our town, mmm?"

I frowned, and my headache grew worse. "I—I trust him."

I can't be wrong about him. I just can't be.

I turned away again when a slight buzz of electricity danced under my skin. Cyrus's question was a valid one. Will had never been specific about his reasons for coming to our town. He'd said he preferred living away from his mother's castle. But what if he'd had another motivation?

I love him, and he loves me. He revealed his secret to me. Why would he betray me? What would he possibly gain from using me? It's not like he could've known that I'd receive these powers from the Goddess.

"Goddess, my head is killing me."

"I'm sorry, Elinor," Skye murmured, and I clenched my jaw.

"There is nothing to be sorry about, Skye. I will find out if he lied to me. I will."

"How do you expect to do that?" Cyrus pushed, and my wolf growled with irritation.

"If he's been lying to you all this time, how will you get him to tell the truth?"

"I just will, okay!" When I turned to face them, Skye's face morphed from worry to fear, and I looked away, forcing my eyes to change back from white. "He said he was going home to find out if his mother knew anything," I said more softly. "That's what he told me. So he'll be back."

But what if you're wrong?

I sighed at that thought. He was a General, a son of the Queen. How could he not know if the Queen was planning something this big? He'd told me about his broken relationship with his mother, but he could have been lying. Everything between us could have been a lie.

Will was the first man I'd ever allowed to get close to me. What if I made a big mistake? I shook my head and walked over to a chair on the other side of the room and sat down. Pinching the bridge of my nose, I took deep breaths to try to calm myself, but it wasn't working.

Will's words from the night he professed his love for me echoed in my mind, and my rapidly beating heart slowed. I focused on the love I'd seen in his eyes and what I'd felt when he'd kissed me. He couldn't have faked all of that. There was no way. I inhaled and sat forward as Cyrus and Skye watched me warily.

"He may have been lying to me—I won't say it's impossible—but I'll wait until he returns to find out. If he's really just been using me, if he's really a spy for the Queen, he'll come back. Until then, there's no sense in jumping to any conclusions."

My head was on the verge of exploding.

"Look, I apologize if I was pushing you just now." Cyrus came over and sat down on the chair across from me. "I know you care about him. I'd be upset too, if someone tried to turn Skye against me simply because I was a demon."

I shrugged, finding it hard to look him in the eye. I couldn't get the memory of what I had almost done to him out of my mind. We'd had no time together before this, but I'd been on edge, not knowing what to say to him. After all, I had almost killed him.

Like the Guards that I'd hurt, he didn't seem to hold my lack of control against me. But I couldn't help feeling guilty every time I thought about how much I must have frightened my own people.

"It's okay," I finally answered.

Skye joined us as well, and Cyrus pulled her onto his lap. I smiled at the loving way they gazed at each other, and I prayed to the Goddess to give me a sign that I wasn't making a big mistake with Will.

If I am *wrong to trust him, wouldn't she have told me?*

I sighed. "Maybe the universe is trying to tell me something."

"About what?" Skye asked. "About Will?"

"Yeah," I drawled, the throbbing at my temples increasing. "Each time we've grown close, something comes between us. What more proof do I need that maybe we aren't meant to be?" I rubbed at my tired eyes.

"Okay, look, maybe I should have kept my mouth shut. I didn't mean to fill you with doubts. I just wanted you to keep an open mind. That is all," Cyrus said.

He looked truly regretful, and I gave him a tight-lipped smile. It was genuine, but it was all I could muster.

"I know. It's just hard to think that after everything that's happened, it was all a lie, you know?" I placed a hand over my chest where I kept the flower that the forest spirit had given to me in the dragon forest. I hadn't even thought about using it while fighting Arden. We had been in a tough spot during that fight, and using the flower to summon help might have been a good idea.

In the end, though, we'd been saved. Will had saved us, and I was glad. I doubted I would have found out that he could walk in the sun otherwise. Not for a while, anyway.

"I understand. I'm not sure how I'd handle it if Cyrus turned against us," Skye added.

Cyrus huffed and made a face. "Excuse me, what? That's not remotely funny."

Skye kissed his forehead. "I wasn't saying you'd actually do that. I'm just saying, I can imagine how conflicted I'd be if I was in Elinor's position. I know you'd never do that, Cyrus. You wouldn't want to make me have to come after you."

They bickered back and forth, something I hadn't heard

them do in far too long. I was busy, however, staring down at my hands. Beneath my fingertips, electricity was buzzing. If I didn't learn to control this new power, Levi would get his way, and I would become an experiment.

"Are you worrying about your divinity?" Cyrus asked.

I looked over at him and saw him looking at my hands. "I never apologized to you."

He shook his head. "You don't need to. What you did, Elinor, was—"

"Incredible." Skye finished the statement for him, and I relaxed my tense arms. "I wish I could have seen you in action."

"I probably would have attacked you, too. I just don't want that to happen again. I need to get a handle on this power."

Skye shrugged. "You will. You always finish what you start, Elinor, once you put your mind to it."

Cyrus smiled devilishly. "Yeah, let's not dwell on the night you almost made everyone shit their pants."

"Gee, thanks. For some reason, that isn't really helping me feel any better about myself."

"I know," he said, sobering up. "But after all, you got your power at the very moment we needed it the most. And sometimes, a little fear is good. It'll give you the extra motivation you need to get your power under control." He pulled Skye closer to him. "Something is coming, and I have a feeling we're all going to need all the strength we can get."

"I guess that means you won't be holding back any longer, huh?"

His lip twitched as he looked at Skye, and she nodded, as if giving him her approval. "Yeah," he answered. "No holding back now. The Vampire Queen's going to die, one way or another."

I wanted revenge, too, for Ms. Clementine, Skye, and all

the other supernaturals who'd been branded and resurrected. But one thought kept echoing through in my mind.

What'll happen to William when she dies?

14

WILL

I entered the dimly lit coven and found it empty of vampires. They were probably sleeping or feeding, and I was thankful for that as I made my way through the house to Vivian's bedroom. I pictured her red hair and ruby eyes, and all I felt was a revulsion that my mother had sent me here in the first place. And even more revulsion that I'd actually gone along with it.

I had spent months living under this roof with a vampire I detested. But that was now coming to an end. I was only here to speak to her and advise her I'd be leaving. Then I'd be on my way.

I'd learned little from my mother, but at least now I knew who was responsible for the killing and reanimation of so many supernaturals. It was surprising to me that she hadn't realized yet what Cain was doing. While her interest was in expanding her domain, it was clear to me that Cain wanted something else. I just needed to find out what.

Nonetheless, I saw the irony in what they were doing, pitting supernaturals against each other and using them to reclaim the land they'd lost. But Cain was also limiting the food supply in the process. He had to see that.

My mother had been right about one thing, though. I had personally contributed to the fear the supernatural community had of vampires. I was not the only savage in vampire history, but I'd been one of the worst. This generation of supernaturals, and the three that came before them, hadn't been alive when my name had driven fear into all who heard it.

I'd terrorized the inhabitants of countless towns and villages, successfully forcing thousands to swear their allegiance to my Queen. It had taken decades, but we were eventually forced into the shadows. The kings and queens before Amythia had kept a peaceful enough relationship with the supernatural and human communities, but when Amythia had gained the throne, she'd wanted to be feared. And it was my greatest shame that I had helped her.

Our obsession with power and control was eventually our undoing. Though it took me a long time, I finally saw that we were poisoning the same world we would have to live in. It was the primary cause of the change I underwent.

My mother didn't care. She wanted to see the world burn. And she was on her way to getting exactly that if she and my brother weren't stopped.

"Will?"

I paused mid-stride and turned to face Vivian.

She frowned as she looked me up and down. "Why are you sneaking around?"

"I was headed to your room."

"Oh? Why? Where have you been?" She walked past me, her deep purple dress dragging behind her, and I remained quiet until we got to her room.

Once inside, I closed the door behind me. "I went home."

Her frown deepened. "Why? Is everything okay?"

"It will be, Vivian," I answered dryly.

Her eyes sharpened. "Did you visit the Queen before or after you went to the Black Souls Market?" When I said nothing, she stared at me with contempt. "You must think I'm a fool."

"You've been watching me?"

She held her hands out. "What choice did you leave me? I'm your fiancée. That's why you came here in the first place, but you're always gone! Since the moment you arrived, you and I have barely spent any time together because you're always off doing who knows what. You are never here, Will, and I needed to know why."

Not good. Not good at all.

"So, when you followed me, did you get the answers you were looking for? Answers you could have asked me for, instead of invading my privacy. Do not forget who I am, Vivian. I don't appreciate being spied on."

She snorted. "Privacy." She sat on her bed, then shook her head slowly, letting her red hair slide forward to shield her face. "I'm to be your bride, Will. Your mother sent you here so that we could bond, and so you could become familiar with my coven. Instead, the distance between us has only grown."

Vivian was loyal to my mother. But if she had learned about Elinor and my involvement with saving her pack, why hadn't she informed the Queen?

"How long?"

She looked up. "How long, what?"

"How long have you been following, Vivian?" I needed to be careful here and remain calm until I knew how much she knew.

She looked away. "Not long. I thought I'd give you your space and allow you some time to warm up to me and the idea of us. But after you left me during that snowstorm a

141

while ago, I knew then that you felt nothing for me." Her red eyes narrowed. "I only followed you once—to the Black Souls Market." She paused. "Why were you there?"

"Why didn't you follow me inside to see for yourself?"

Her eyes turned into slits. "Maybe I did, Will. So I'd advise you to stop speaking to me as if I were a fucking child! Something's been going on with you, and I want to know what!"

No, she hadn't followed me inside. Vivian wouldn't set foot inside that market because as strong and cunning as she was, she was also sheltered. She was nothing more than just a privileged vampire girl, allowed to play with supernaturals and humans as if they were toys. During one of my strolls through the house, I found a room where the rotting bodies of humans had been left.

My eyes turned red, and I struggled to control my anger. "Did you know about the Queen's plans for the supernaturals?"

She looked confused for a moment, then her face morphed into an expression of amusement. Before long, she was cackling loudly, her head dropping as she laughed long and hard. I didn't move or speak. If I did, I was afraid I'd kill her. Her voice sounded like the scratching of nails on a wall, and I couldn't stand it any longer. She was an insolent creature who I could clearly see would only grow worse as she grew older.

Vampires like her were the worst kind of creature. They'd cause havoc simply for entertainment without caring about the negative impact on anyone else. The fact that I saw bits of my past self in her made me dislike her even more.

"The Queen didn't tell you? Oh, how you've fallen from grace." She wiped at a tear. "Well, I suppose you didn't really need to know, did you? She sent you here to court me, but we both know how that's been going. And honestly, now I'm not so mad about it. I thought you were her favorite. But I was wrong."

"You've been wrong about a lot of things, Vivian, including your purpose."

Even if I hadn't met Elinor, I wouldn't have married this woman. She was my mother's choice, not mine.

She went still, and her usually pleasant face changed to reveal the real her—the sinister monster she truly was, not the sweet woman she pretended to be. I found it odd that she even tried to keep up that façade with me. There were gentle enough vampires around—they weren't all savages—but she wasn't one of them.

Her eyes grew murderous. "What happened to you, Will? You're nothing like the man I heard about, the warrior who struck fear wherever he went." She looked me up and down with disgust. "As intimidating as you are, you're nothing like that man. So maybe they were all just stories. You're weak, Will, and you're growing weaker. There's no way you'll be King."

The control I'd been trying so hard to keep finally broke, and I moved toward her. Her eyes widened when I vanished from where I was standing, and she gasped as I grabbed her face from behind and bent her head. My fangs sank into her throat like a knife slicing through butter. My hand muffled her scream, and as her blood flowed into my mouth, I pulled away and threw her across the room.

Her wooden dresser cracked beneath her and her hand flew to her neck as she got on her knees. Black veins crawled up her skin, her black blood pouring out on the floor. Her hand was shaking as she pulled it away from her neck, a look of panic on her face. Unlike other vampires, blood coursed through my veins, but the rest of my kind had a black liquid in place of blood.

"I'm not healing!"

143

"There are things you don't know about me, things that might have been left out of the stories you've been told. A vampire's venom rarely affects another vampire . . . but mine does. And my bite is lethal. But you're lucky. I only gave you a low dose of venom, just enough to block your healing receptors."

My body was almost shaking with excitement at the smell of her fear. The look on her face of utter dread, as if I were a monster, was filling me with pure ecstasy.

My venom was another reason I had been so greatly feared by other vampires. But after our kind had been banished to the current Vampire Territory and my legend had faded, the Queen made sure that this particular detail faded as well. It would only give those who hated me more reason to believe I wasn't one of them.

But the man I once was crawled closer to the surface with each step I took towards her. Images from my past, things I'd placed in a box and locked away, surfaced in my mind, and I closed my eyes for a moment. I needed to remain in control, or things would get out of hand. My gums were aching to pierce flesh, and when my eyes opened again, Vivian was on her feet and backing away from me, her hand still on her neck.

"It's been so long since I've smelled such sweet fear." I looked down at my hands, the warmth in them fading as I changed into my vampire form.

My skin turned gray, and I bent my neck to the side, the bones cracking as black veins appeared up my arms along with my neck and mouth. "You're a fool to think the Queen would be so adamant to have me as her successor if I was weak. There has never been a vampire like me, and there never will be again." I stopped walking towards her. "I should kill you now and be done with it."

"Will, please—"

I blinked out of sight and reappeared before her, pressing a finger to her lips. Her body quivered in fear, and I couldn't stop a grin from crossing my face. She deserved this. "The venom will fade soon, and you'll heal again."

My finger on her lips moved to her chin, and I tipped her head back. "If I was still the vampire I used to be, I would have killed you long ago, just so I wouldn't have to hear your voice. You can forget about becoming royalty. This engagement is off."

Her lips parted, and I swiftly covered her mouth with my hand. I tsked as I shook my head and bent her head to the side. Her hand covering her wound clamped down on her neck further, and I sighed. I wasn't going to bite her again. I didn't need more of her blood in my system. During sex, feasting on another vampire's blood could be enticing, but any other time, I found the taste repulsive.

I released her and turned away to leave. My thirst for blood was growing, and the last thing I wanted to do was kill a human or supernatural on sight.

Or be on the verge of losing control when I saw Elinor.

I growled. I'd have to feed before going to see her because the last thing I wanted was to scare her off. Telling Elinor my mother was behind her friend's abduction and that friend's mother's murder wouldn't be easy. Loyalty meant everything to me, and if I helped Elinor and the other supernaturals, I'd be betraying my Queen, my mother.

But I couldn't let her continue with her crazy plan.

I also was afraid that in the time I'd been gone, Elinor might have grown suspicious of me. And considering my mother was behind it all, I wouldn't blame her if she did. There was a foul taste in my mouth, and it had nothing to do with Vivian's blood.

In the end, whether or not I told Elinor the truth, I would have to stop my mother. One way or another, I'd have to put an end to her plans. The world she was trying to create wasn't one I wanted to live in. And I'd be damned if she used me as a reason for doing it. I hadn't asked her to kill everyone just to expand our domain. Hell, I didn't want the throne to begin with.

But I knew I had to tell Elinor and let the chips land where they would. The werewolves were going to discover the truth eventually, and she would definitely question my loyalty if she learned of my mother's involvement from someone else.

"You can't do this!" Vivian cried as I got to the door. "You can't do this to me! I'm to be Queen! Me!"

"I can't? I just did, Vivian. Now run along and tell the Queen. We both know you will."

"You'll fucking pay for this, Will. I swear it!"

I glided my tongue over my fangs and glanced at her over my shoulder. "All you need to do is give me a reason, Vivian, and I'll thoroughly enjoy showing you the man I used to be. You know nothing of cruelty. You're a child. If you'd like to live out the rest of your pathetic life, I suggest you be a good girl and stay away from me."

Her mouth clamped shut.

15

CYRUS

"*J*'ll help you with that." I held my hands out to a werewolf carrying a bundle of folded towels.

She stopped and looked at me hesitantly before glancing at Darian, who stood behind me. I wasn't offended. I was a demon, after all, and the Blackmoon Pack was the only one to have welcomed a dark creature like me to live among them. Wolves from other packs still found my presence unnerving.

Darian and I, along with six other Guards, had arrived to help this pack two hours ago, after visiting the other one that had been attacked first. The damage to this pack wasn't as severe as the previous one. Although there'd been more Guards with the other pack, they were up against a greater number of reanimated supernaturals. In the end, it had been a bloody mess. This pack was smaller, but there'd been fewer resurrected supernaturals to fight. The first pack's Guards had killed off many of them before they'd been overrun.

Luna Clarice had ordered us to take supplies such as food and medicine to both packs, and we'd left five Guards with the first pack to help in any way they could. Both Alphas told

Darian the same story. Out of the blue, the resurrected supernaturals had gone on a rampage. They hadn't been looking for anything in particular—they'd just wanted to kill.

They burned down homes and murdered as many wolves as they could before leaving as quickly as they had arrived. They took several wolves, as well, and I knew exactly what would become of them. I stopped and handed a towel to a woman who was comforting a small girl—no more than five years old—as she cried over a covered body on the ground. There were two rows of shrouded bodies, eleven in total, laid out for survivors to check for missing family members.

The woman carrying the towels beside me sniffled as she made her way to the pack house. "There was no warning. They attacked us so suddenly, we couldn't react. We had heard about what happened to the Blackmoon Pack, but still, we weren't prepared."

"How many wolves did they take?"

She shrugged, her blue eyes rimmed red. "Six are confirmed to be missing—two of them only teen pups."

"Was there someone among them who seemed to have been controlling the supernaturals?"

She shook her head as we entered the pack house. "No. But they all stopped fighting at the exact same moment."

"Did you notice any vampires?"

She looked thoughtful for a moment, then shook her head and adjusted the towels in her arms. "I don't remember seeing any. There might have been. I—I'm only a cook that works in the kitchen. I barely survived, myself."

There were bruises on her arms and bags under her eyes, but she was still doing what she could to help. "Thank you for your help. I didn't catch your name," she said.

"Cyrus," I told her.

"I'm Sabrina." She took the rest of the towels from me and

began handing them out among the wounded being treated on the floor.

I stood there for a moment, watching her work alongside the other wolves and the elderly wolf who appeared to be the pack's doctor. Unlike our pack, these wolves didn't have a second location to go to. They were all terrified that they'd be attacked again. If they didn't die in the battle, they risked being captured and becoming one of the mindless creatures attacking their own.

I winced as my right arm burned, and I pulled my sleeve up. One of my tattoos was bright red, so I turned and walked out of the house. My eyes scanned the wolves outside until I finally spotted Darian.

"I need to go. Someone's trying to use my portal."

"How do you know?" He placed a large log he was carrying to the pack house kitchen on the ground.

I showed him the demonic symbol on my forearm, and he nodded, his eyes narrowing curiously. We'd learned nothing of importance, so getting away wouldn't be a problem for me. Unlike Connor, who was sometimes friendly, Darian was a little more standoffish. As the leader of the Guards for the Blackmoon Pack, he always wore his uniform, even when off duty. Connor was the pack's Beta, but both men seemed to do the same job when Darian wasn't out on missions.

"Go. I'll stay here tonight. Connor went back to the other pack. So once you're done, return to our pack, okay?"

I nodded as my wings appeared, and a few shocked gasps met my ears. I pushed off the ground, my wings flapping loudly. Now was the worst possible time for this to happen.

The portal was close to the Blackmoon Pack in a small cave hidden in the woods. Drawn to the portal's power, the whispering voices of spirits trapped on Earth could be heard at the entrance to the cave.

I made my way deep inside the cave until I reached the

pulsing red light of the portal. While the cave's walls were all stone, the portal looked like a thin layer of skin with black lines running through it. Circling it were symbols I'd engraved into the rock to keep the portal sealed.

I placed my hand against the entrance. The burning sensation in my hand vanished as a tear appeared and I pushed through. The symbol carved into my hand was the only way to access the portal. Otherwise, it would repel the person or demon trying to use it.

On the other side, the cave continued. The intense magical energy of the Demon Realm fell over me like a weighted blanket. I expected to find a demon or a lost soul trying to use the portal. Instead, I saw my mother.

She sat on a chair made of gold with her legs crossed as two incubi guards stood like statues behind her. She was inspecting her nails but looked up with a smile as I stopped before her.

"Hello, son. You certainly took your time getting here."

"I'm busy, Mother. What's the meaning of this?"

"So, no 'Hi, Mother. How are you, Mother? I've missed you, Mother'?"

I stared at her unblinkingly, and she sighed and got up. She flicked her silky black hair over her shoulder before waving her hand at her guards. "Leave."

They turned and left immediately, and I allowed her to pull me into a hug, as a floating orb of light above us illuminated the dark cave. She released me, looking me over before frowning. Since my last visit to the Demon Realm after I'd killed the adracsas bounty hunter my brother had sent after me, I hadn't seen her.

I hadn't missed her, him, or the Demon Realm. If it had been up to me, I'd never return.

"You look tired." Her frown deepened. "And you look

pale. Why do you always look so pale, Cyrus? You need to feed!"

"Mother, I have a lot going on right now. Why did you try to use my portal?"

"Because it was the only way I'd get to speak to you. I knew you wouldn't come if I summoned you."

Well, she isn't wrong about that.

I inhaled deeply. "Okay, I'm here now."

Her hand on my cheek fell to her side, and her eyes drained of vitality. I tried not to react, but my brows knitted at how genuinely sad she looked. My mother was a talented actress— I'd learned that a long time ago. But at times like this, it was hard to tell if she was sincere or not. I'd always been her prized son, her offspring with the Demon King who would forever bring her glory. Could it be that I meant something more?

"Do you truly despise me so much, Cyrus? All I want for you is glory—when you take over my Legion and take your place as the Demon King's son."

It wasn't wise for me to answer. I didn't despise my mother, but I didn't trust her either. And I didn't care about glory one bit. As for being the Demon King's son, I'd only spoken to the man once—a one-sided conversation where he told me I only had three years to remain on Earth. Not exactly a memory I cherished.

That bastard.

When I made no move to respond, she shook her head and turned away to sit down once more. "I heard about what's happening on Earth."

"And? I figured you'd be happy about it all."

She shrugged and looked down at her nails. "Mmm, I am. It's entertaining, to be honest, but—" She looked up at me from under her lashes. "I want to help you."

"Why would you want to do that?"

"Because if anything happens to your precious little wolves, you won't return. And I can't have you defying your father's command. No matter how much you hate him, you can't anger him. Even you are wise enough to know that."

"I'll return as he commands, Mother. You don't need to worry."

Her eyes hardened as she placed her hands on both arms of the chair. "I do have to worry when there's a good chance you'll get hurt."

That piqued my interest, and I stepped forward. "What do you mean?"

"You know by now that the Vampire Queen is the one building an army, yes?"

I nodded.

"Good. Then I have information you might find interesting about her and the origin of her kind."

I shook my head. "I don't need a history lesson on the origins of vampires. I need to know how to defeat her."

"Sometimes, to understand how to end something, you have to know how it began, Cyrus." She leaned forward. "To know how to kill her, you have to know how she came into being."

"I understand." I exhaled exasperatedly. We needed to have this conversation quickly. Time passed differently in the Demon Realm, and I needed to get back to Earth before too much time went by there. "I'm listening, and thank you for the help."

She paused for a moment, as if in shock that I thanked her. She looked away, deep in thought, then turned back to me. "You're related to her."

I went still. "What?"

"She's a descendant of the Demon King, Cyrus. You're related to the Vampire Queen."

I heard her words, but I felt like I wasn't hearing her

correctly. "How is she a descendant of the Demon King? She's a vampire."

She inhaled deeply, and anger flashed in her eyes. "The Demon King had a child with a goddess a very long time ago. The child was . . . different—a mutant. She started out as a hideous thing, but as she grew, her body changed."

I leaned against the wall of the cave as my mother spoke, and I wondered if she had known that child.

"She became incredibly beautiful, but she was still a mutant. Her bite could turn demons into creatures that were either like you and me in appearance, or bloodthirsty things that killed everything." She looked my way. "She challenged your father, so he banished her to your Earth."

"Please tell me you're joking. The Vampire Queen is my great, great, great—" I paused because I had no idea how to calculate the vampire generations that had passed, and there were too many greats to bother saying anyways. "She's my great-grandniece?"

"Yes," she answered bluntly. I pressed a finger to my temple. "You can't be the one who kills her, and it has nothing to do with the fact that she's your great-grandniece. No one on Earth can kill her."

I frowned. "Why not? There has to be a way to stop her. She's building an army, and the way things are going, supernaturals and humans are going to be wiped out."

She stood up and snapped her fingers. "I just told you why no one can kill her, Cyrus. She's a descendant of a goddess and the Demon King. That means she has divinity—and a lot of it. Only a god can kill her. And considering gods don't walk the earth anymore, good luck finding one."

I instantly thought of Elinor. Was this the reason the Goddess activated her dormant divinity? Elinor wasn't a goddess, but she clearly possessed an immense amount of divinity. Would it be enough to kill the Queen?

"What is it?" my mother asked inquisitively, and I shook my head.

"Nothing," I grumbled back. The last thing I was going to do was tell my mother about Elinor. "I'm thinking. Why didn't my father kill her? His power is similar to that of a god. He's just not allowed in the God Realm. He could have killed his daughter if she was such an abomination."

She shrugged. "I don't know."

From the way she bit down on her lip, I could tell she was lying. Maybe he hadn't been able to kill her because the girl was his own child. Even though I considered my father heartless, there was a chance he'd cared about that girl. Still, I couldn't see my father allowing someone who'd been creating problems for him to go without punishment. And being banished to another world wasn't much of a sentence, in my eyes.

Especially because he'd left her to run rampant on Earth, birthing more vampires.

I turned to leave, and my mother grabbed my arm. "Cyrus, wait." When I turned to her, her hold on my arm grew tighter. "This isn't your fight, Cyrus. You can't face her, and she won't spare you if she finds out who you are to her. Come home."

"I can't do that," I told her softly and gently pulled my hand away. "Earth has been my home for years, and I can't leave now. We'll find a way to kill her."

"And if you can't?"

We already had a start. "Don't worry about it, okay? I'll return to the Demon Realm soon enough, but not before I'm ready."

Elinor

154

I focused on the sound of drums playing in my head. The traditional werewolf anthem was helping to soothe my jittery nerves as I walked through the forest. There was a slight chill in the air as the day drew closer to an end, with the sun already disappearing over the horizon.

I'd ventured into the forest last night, but Will hadn't appeared, which had made the already edgy state I was in worse.

I needed answers, and I needed them now.

My thoughts were split into two factions, one side battling the other. On one side, I feared that Will had betrayed me. All evidence pointed in that direction. But on the other hand, I remembered our moments together, moments when I truly believed he cared for me, and I couldn't help giving him the benefit of the doubt. I hated being so unsure. It wasn't like me.

I lowered myself onto the grass and inhaled the salty air drifting up from the sea. It had been a long time since I'd come to this cliff, but the moment I sat down, the gentle wind and the bright sunset brought me the sense of peace and relaxation I'd been craving for days.

My tense shoulders slumped. I crossed my legs at the ankles, then placed my hands behind me to prop myself up. I held my head back and closed my eyes, recalling the night Connor had caught Will and me at this very spot. Even now, with the help of a little compulsion from Will, Connor still thought he saw me almost slip over the edge of the cliff—not kiss a vampire.

Connor had been one of my guardians since I was a child, and I wondered what he'd say if he ever remembered what he really saw that day. Then I thought of my nemesis, Darian. While Connor's personality was laid back and observant,

Darian was a Werewolf Guard, hard-headed and stubborn. I knew he'd lose his mind at the mere mention of me being with a vampire.

Well, they were all eventually going to be in for a treat.

The sound of footsteps approaching made me jump to my feet quickly. But my excitement withered and died when I saw Faelen.

"Hi. You seem a little jumpy tonight."

"You startled me, that's all."

"You also don't look very happy to see me."

Apparently I wasn't doing a very good job of hiding my emotions. My eyes scanned the forest behind her as she walked over to stand by my side.

With her eyes on the sea, she said, "He's not there."

I froze. "Excuse me?"

"Will. He hasn't arrived yet." She turned to face me. "That's who you're looking for, right?"

I wasn't sure if I should answer or not. She clearly already knew about Will, but why should I confirm anything? Sure, we had a mutual enemy—Levi—but she was an Enchanted, a werewolf. She could tell someone about Will and me, and then I'd have an even bigger problem on my hands.

"Relax, Elinor, I won't tell anyone. I was in your mind, remember? I saw enough to know that you're in love with a vampire." She held her hands up. "I wasn't prying around in your memories. Some of your thoughts were just really loud."

"Aren't you going to tell me how crazy I am to have fallen for a vampire?"

She continued to stare ahead, her white hair blowing in the wind. "It's none of my business who you love, but I do think you need to be careful." She turned to me then, her eyes wandering back and forth across my face. "Your safety is a priority right now."

"Will has saved my life many times, Faelen. You don't need to worry about my safety with him."

"Except . . . how do we know that him saving you wasn't part of some greater plan concocted by his mother?"

I sighed loudly and turned to face the sea. This wasn't a conversation I wanted to have again. I already hashed it out with Cyrus. I understood that there was a possibility that Will had been playing me this whole time.

I knew all of that, and I didn't need a reminder.

"I get it, okay? And that's why I'm waiting for him here. So he can tell me the truth."

She said nothing in response, but I could see her still staring at me from my peripheral vision. "I didn't mean to upset you or to be insensitive to what you might be feeling right now, but this is something you need to hear. Right now, Elinor, you represent the best chance we have for survival against these reanimated supernaturals. Your life and safety are a top priority."

"What does that have to do with Will?"

"At the end of the day, he's a vampire. He might be a special one, but he's still a vampire. You need to be prepared if he chooses his kind over you. The Goddess chose you, Elinor. She has a plan for you. What'll you do if you have no choice but to choose your people over the man you love? What will you do?"

She stared at me for a moment, as if she were waiting for an answer, then walked away. I wrapped my arms around myself as the world suddenly felt cold. I didn't have an answer for her because I didn't want to think about that, not now. I didn't know what I'd do if Will chose his kind over me. And if he appeared to me tonight and revealed that everything between us was a lie . . . well, I didn't think I could take that. Not after everything else that had happened.

But I might have to decide—would I just let him go, or

would I fight him and turn him over to my father for questioning?

Choices. We all had choices to make in life. But killing the man I loved, or turning him over to be killed, wasn't a choice I'd ever dreamed I'd have to make.

16

VAMPIRE QUEEN AMYTHIA

*M*y fist went through the wall, shattering it. But I barely felt the impact, and my rage only grew worse as I punched another hole, then another. I could hear footsteps scurrying away down the hall. Someone was wise enough to know when to make themselves scarce.

I was livid!

William was the future of this race, even if he hated the idea of it. I placed a hand on my stomach and hissed as I walked down the hall to my chamber. Even without royal blood, he was blessed with a talent no other vampire had. His strength almost equaled that of a royal, and he had a soul. He'd taken my gift of vampirism and turned it into something evolutionary. He was the future of vampirism—if my efforts ever came to fruition.

He and Cain meant everything to me. And while Cain was loyal and had remained by my side, William was so special—in every way—that I tended to overlook his outbursts. He would bring about a new age for vampires . . . if the experiments I'd conducted in secret ever showed some promise. Though I was optimistic on that front, I hadn't received any good news lately from the dark witches who worked for me.

I felt certain William could sire children naturally instead of relying on his bite the way I'd had to. I'd tried over the centuries to create life using his sperm. Little did he know that Levia had secretly kept me supplied. Unfortunately, she'd ruined that when she sided against William, forcing me to send human slaves to seduce him. But he was as stubborn as they came, and at the time, he'd only slaughtered them. Even when he'd kept humans and other supernaturals as pets, he never slept with them. He only engaged in sexual relationships with other vampires.

My nails dug into my palms with frustration as I continued down the hall. The vampires who walked by me kept their eyes down and hurried past me. I was aware I was in my vampire form, my skin gray and my fangs on display. William was so blind to the gift he possessed, and sometimes it drove me mad.

Only royals could reproduce, but over the centuries, I'd tried and failed countless times, forcing me to create Cain and William from my bite only. There were three vampires that I'd turned recently, but they were still newborns. And because I turned them, they were more feral than normal newborns. Those three were now in cocoons until William inherited the throne. Then he'd have three Generals for himself.

With my venom flowing through their veins, their thirst for blood would be insatiable. Sometimes, it drove them insane, which was why vampires I turned myself often died. Their bodies, whether human or supernatural, were not always strong enough to handle the change.

And not every vampire I'd turned became a General. The ones with abilities that weren't violent enough made up the Council that assisted me in governing my people.

Sighing, I walked into my chamber as the guards positioned on either side of the door pushed them open.

"Send a human and a fae to me."

"Yes, my Queen," they both answered in unison before closing the door behind them.

William's words replayed over and over in my mind, leaving me in a state of constant irritation. When had he become so detached from us? From me? He was almost unrecognizable to me now, and I hated that, but I knew forcing him to return to the castle to live wouldn't work. I wasn't sure what had happened to him, what had changed him so drastically, but I missed the man who had once ruled by my side as if he were King. Cain had been born first, but William had quickly surpassed him. Still, Cain remained the more cunning of the two.

If William had been anyone else, if he hadn't been so special, I would have killed him long ago for his insolence, for turning his back on his Queen and his people. But then, they had also turned their backs on him. Perhaps that was why he'd changed. I wasn't blind or deaf to what they said about him, but he'd always handled their hatred well.

Or so I had thought.

I understood their jealousy, as even I coveted his gifts. Some vampires, young ones, could remember what it had been like to walk in the sun before they were turned, but not me. Born in and to the darkness, I would forever dwell in it —unless I discovered how to gain William's ability. And it wasn't like I hadn't tried over the years. After many failed experiments where I consumed his blood and my body promptly rejected it, I was forced to admit defeat on that front.

But despite my failure to improve my own personal abilities, I still had high hopes for the future evolution of our kind—hopes that rested with William. Perhaps I'd never walk in the sun, but if I succeeded in making it so my people could, I'd be remembered forever as a legend—the Queen who brought about a new era of vampire domination. For if vampires could roam freely, day or night, we would dominate the world.

Maybe that was the difference between the other vampires and myself—how we saw William. For them, he was a constant reminder of all they'd lost from their former lives. For me, he represented hope and possibilities. A new beginning. My legacy.

So when Cain devised his new plan as a way to control the supernaturals, I'd happily agreed to it. It fit right into my ultimate plans for William and our new beginning for all vampire-kind. Humans and supernaturals had governed the earth long enough. Why should I be satisfied with the small box they'd shoved us into?

There was a time when we'd lived as free as they were now, when we weren't starving. I wanted to walk the earth again and smell the fear flowing from everyone I passed. I stepped onto my balcony and looked up at the dark, cloudy sky. This land had died long ago, and the air, rank with blood and death, was more beautiful to me than a forest filled with trees. Darkness, endless darkness, was all I'd ever known. If I was forced to live in it forever, then everyone else would share the same fate.

I'd see to that.

I remained where I was on the balcony as my guards returned with a human and a fae. I inhaled deeply, smelling their fear—reveling in it. Drinking it in like a fine glass of wine. As the adrenaline coursed through their bodies and caused their panicked hearts to beat ever faster, I wouldn't be surprised if they died from the fear alone.

This was the way things should be.

Striking fear into the hearts of others was real power. I

gazed down at my hands as black veins appeared beneath my pale skin. Walking back into the room, I removed my dress, leaving myself bare before the guards and the two captives.

My guards stared at me with lust and awe while the human woman and male fae continued to shiver with fear.

"Shhh," I hushed them as I walked forward. "Guards, leave us."

The guards turned and left the room as my skin returned to its normal pale color and my fangs vanished. I caressed the woman's freshly washed blonde hair as I admired the green eyes of the fae. They were both naked and had been bathed before being brought here. There was nothing better than making my prey truly mine, feasting on their blood when they were filled with ecstasy and then rolling in that blood, suddenly tainted with fear, as I slaughtered them.

Three hours with my lovely pets passed in the blink of an eye for me, though I recognized it was probably not so for them. Time meant nothing to me the way it did to the now-dead human and the fae male lying beside me in bed. Killing the human had been easy, but I'd wanted to keep the fae alive a little longer.

I rolled onto my side and threw a leg over his naked torso as blood continued to flow from wounds covering his body. I trailed kisses up his shoulder and chest before climbing on top of him, blood dripping from my hair with every movement.

"Do you want me to kill you?"

Nodding his head apparently took effort, and he began coughing, causing blood to splatter over his lips.

"I hadn't planned on ripping your tongue out. That was an accident. I got a little . . . overzealous. You are a most enticing treat. I want you to know that."

More tears slipped from his beautiful eyes, and I pouted as I leaned forward to rest my weight on his chest.

"Oh, I know. I know it hurts, but I like your eyes, and I've always enjoyed the taste of fae blood." I sighed. "There was someone I spent moments like this with often, but that was so long ago."

He began coughing again, and I covered his mouth with my hand. "Do you have children? I do. I have two sons who are incredible men, but the one I used to enjoy moments like this with has lost his way."

I sat up, my core gently rubbing against his stomach. "He'll find his way back, though. So I think I'll have you healed until then. He'll enjoy you, too."

A knock came at the door, and my hair fanned out around me like a thousand snakes. "What?"

The door opened slowly, and a guard poked his head instead. "Your Majesty, I'm sorry to interrupt you, but I have important news. There's been a sighting of . . . a white wolf."

My body went stiff at the mention of a white wolf—my only real weakness. I hadn't thought they still existed.

"Come in." I climbed off the bed, the fae beneath me temporarily forgotten, and the guard entered the room, his head bowed in respect. "Tell me."

"Your resurrected army attacked several wolf packs, but one pack was under the protection of a white wolf, a young girl named Elinor. From the report I received, she can command lightning. She killed all the supernaturals we sent."

I turned my back to hide my reaction. I couldn't allow him to see my fear.

"I thought they didn't exist anymore," I muttered to myself. "Are you certain she was a white wolf?"

"Yes, my Queen. She, along with two demons, attacked a facility holding the abducted supernaturals as well, forcing them to relocate."

White wolves were the only creatures strong enough to kill a vampire with royal blood, but they were rare now—

almost mythical. A white wolf was responsible for the deaths of my parents and all the royals before them. Without the ability to give birth, the royal bloodline would end with me, but I was fine with that. A new age was coming under William's rule, and who knew what could happen?

My jaw clenched as I walked away, leaving a trail of blood on the floor in my wake. Still, I wasn't planning on dying any time soon.

It had been centuries since I last saw a white wolf, or even heard of one existing.

Just then, Cain entered the room, and I narrowed my eyes at him. "You didn't tell me that someone found a facility. That's why you suggested attacking werewolf packs instead of using the same method we'd been using for months! You knew of this white wolf and said nothing to me!"

Cain's eyes slid to the guard.

"Do not think of punishing him. He was right to come to me. You may leave." The guard hurried from the room, and I vanished from where I stood, reappearing in front of Cain seconds later. The slap I gave him across the face echoed through the room. "You knew of a white wolf, and you thought to keep it a secret from me? Explain yourself!"

"I wanted to find her and bring her to you, my Queen, that's all. I didn't want to worry you until I had the situation under control."

"Worry me?" I yelled. "Do you think a vampire as powerful as I am should be worried about a little wolf?"

He lowered his head. "I only meant that a white wolf is the only creature alive that could actually kill you. I didn't want you to be concerned about it until I had the wolf in my possession." He looked up at me. "She'd be an asset if turned, I'm sure."

I walked away and grabbed the leg of the fae, pulling him to the edge of the bed. My fangs buried themselves in his neck, emptying him of the last of his blood before allowing him to fall to the floor.

Enchanteds were useful when turned—because of their divinity, their powers remained, though they were typically diminished. White wolves possessed much more divinity than Enchanteds. This Elinor would undoubtedly keep most, if not all, of her power after turning.

I already had William. What would happen if I could turn this wolf and make her mine as well? She'd make him an ideal wife and rule by his side. I thought of the union—and hopefully the children being born to it—and smiled.

Power, so much power!

I had originally intended to order Cain to find and kill her, but now I saw what a mistake that would have been. "Find her," I told him, my excitement returning quickly. "Take her alive and with minimal harm. We're going to make a few changes to our plans."

Cyrus

*E*veryone was silent. I looked around at the people I loved and could see the shock on their faces. Their expressions were probably not far from what mine had been when my mother had told me about my connection to the Vampire Queen. I could see the slow realization on Elinor's face soon morph into uncertainty and then panic. If a being with divinity—and enough of it—was the only one capable of killing the Queen, then Elinor was the only one among us strong enough to take on the task.

Now we knew the truth—this was her real purpose.

"I can't believe she's your great-grandniece," Skye whispered beside me, and I shook my head in response.

"She's nothing to me, Skye. Nothing."

Luna Clarice looked worried, and her hands clenched on her lap while Alpha Grayson looked contemplative. But I could see that it worried him, too. Any parent would be worried if their child had just been given the burden Elinor now had to bear. A great responsibility rested on her shoulders, but she wouldn't be alone. She'd need all the help she could get from us to get her to the Queen.

Levi had contacted Faelen, confirming that the Council approved launching an attack on the Queen, but Elinor would have to work harder to get control of her power. He also insisted that the only way we could move forward with that attack was if we could rally the other races first.

At least that bought us some time.

The last members of the pack would leave soon, followed by the Alpha and Luna, and Elinor would go to a secure location with Skye and Darian. Theanos hadn't returned, but if the dragons agreed to help us—which was unlikely, but possible—we'd have a considerable advantage over the vampires. Even one dragon would be good.

"Elinor? You understand, don't you?" Clarice leaned forward.

Elinor looked at her mother and nodded. "Yes," she answered, taking a deep breath. "You all believe I am the only one who can do this."

"If the Goddess intervened to give you these powers, she must have believed it too," Faelen said.

Elinor pressed a finger to her temple. Then she suddenly blurted out, "But I can't do it. I can't." She got up and walked away, running a hand through her hair.

"I understand how you must feel, Elinor, but—"

Elinor spun on her heel, her eyes flashing white, and Faelen froze. "I'm sorry, Faelen, but do you really? Do any of you understand what you're asking of me? I've never been the kind of girl who sat on the sidelines, but this is something else. You're telling me I, specifically, have to be the one to kill the Vampire Queen." She shook her head, obviously still in shock.

"And why not you?" Faelen argued. "In war, anything can happen. If the Goddess willed it, even a human could end the Queen." She walked over to Elinor and said softly, "What if the circumstances were as we first thought, and anyone could kill the Queen? What would you have done if you'd found yourself in the position to deliver the final blow? You'd have had no choice but to act. So why does knowing for certain that you're the one who has to do it change things for you?"

"Because now everyone will expect me to get it done. If I fail, it'll be on me! If I die and she lives, I will have doomed us all."

"You won't be doing this alone, Elinor," Alpha Grayson said, and Elinor's eyes returned to their natural color. "You won't be going to the Vampire Territory alone. We'll all be there, fighting alongside you, helping to put you in the position you need to be in to fulfill your duty."

She took a deep breath but remained standing, her face red as her eyes darted from one person to the next. No one spoke for a moment, and in my mind, I could hear my mother's words repeating that this wasn't my fight. I was still the son of the Demon King and a Sin. Even without divinity needed to kill the Queen, I could still fight beside Elinor and have her back.

"You're doing it again," I said to her. "Doubting yourself. You need to have faith in your power and trust that everyone will do everything they can to get you to the Queen. You just can't be hesitant about this."

"I think, right now, I need to be, Cyrus."

I shook my head. "No. Right now, you need to trust your

power. You fear it, fear hurting one of us or someone else you care about. But if you keep thinking like that, you'll never learn control. I feared my power for a time, but I realized it wasn't going anywhere, and if I didn't learn to control it, it would control me. I'm still learning—" Blue flames appeared at my fingertips. "—but I'm open to it."

"We also don't know when the Queen will release all the supernaturals she's resurrected. Heck, we don't even know how many there are," Skye pointed out, and Elinor sat back down. "We need to act . . . before she does."

Reports were coming in of attacks on other species from the resurrected supernaturals, though the goal appeared to be capturing more supernaturals over killing them. The Queen was obviously still building her army. We also didn't know what her end goal was. Before we lost more people, we needed to talk the other supernaturals into joining forces. Now that we had someone strong enough to take out the Queen, it should be easier to do.

"Darian will be with you when you leave," Alpha Grayson said to Elinor. "He'll be able to teach you and quickly." Elinor made a face, and her father crossed his arms over his chest. "I know, he's not your favorite teacher, but he's the only one you've got."

"It's just a lot to process," Elinor grumbled to herself. "I might have divinity, but I don't have the time to learn the control I'm going to need."

"Then trust the Goddess," Faelen replied. "Pray to her and ask for strength and guidance. She'll give it to you. She already has."

"You've been eager to become a Guard, eager to protect the pack. And now, you've got the opportunity." Alpha Grayson leaned forward, his voice low but filled with finality. "I'm sorry you don't have any choice about this. It's just the way things are. So ground yourself, accept what is . . . and end this. For all of us."

Elinor's eyes hardened, her father's words apparently getting through to her, and she nodded her head firmly. I understood that she felt she wasn't ready. It was the same way I felt about becoming the next Sin, Lust. I didn't have a choice either.

Her eyes rimmed red with tears, Luna Clarice abruptly stood and left the room. Alpha Grayson sighed, then got up and followed his wife. "I'll talk to her."

When he left, Elinor placed her hands on her knees and leaned forward, obviously trying to think her way through this. "I'll ask Will how to get into the Queen's castle. That'll save some time. Then all I'll have to do is find her. Hopefully, she won't join the fight, and I'll be able to corner her in a room somewhere."

"Wait, hold on." Skye sent a hesitant look Faelen's way, then glanced back at Elinor.

"She knows about him. It's fine," Elinor clarified.

"Yes, I know about the vampire. And while that's a good idea, Elinor, I believe you need to speak to Will first. We still don't know if we can trust him."

Elinor sat up, but her eyes remained on the floor. Faelen was right, but I doubted Elinor needed to be told that again. I could tell she felt very conflicted about Will right now, and I felt for her. It must have been horrible caring for Will while, at the same time, not feeling totally convinced she could trust him.

"I also think it would be wise if we all leave tomorrow night," Faelen added. "The last group of wolves will head out then, and we need to do the same. Especially you, Elinor. News about your powers will have traveled fast. Somehow, I doubt the Queen is unaware that a white wolf has the power to kill her. When she finds out you exist, she'll be coming for you."

Skye stood up to leave, and I did the same. "If only we could do something now, so we'd have the element of surprise working in our favor."

"Yeah," Elinor drawled.

Skye walked over to her. "You can do this," she said, holding her hands out.

Elinor slid her hands into Skye's, and they both inhaled and exhaled at the same time. The bond between them was beautiful. They fed each other strength when it was needed. Although Theanos and I were close, we weren't that close, and a part of me wished that hadn't been that way.

Opening up to my family just wasn't easy for me. Not even with Theanos.

17

ELINOR

$\mathcal{I}$ was happy to be back in a Guard's uniform. This one had been created just for me, so it fit me like a glove. I ran a hand down the twisting black line on my arm signifying the pack I was from and smiled. While I wasn't an official Guard, when I gazed down at the ring on my left middle finger, I couldn't help feeling proud.

I didn't smile for long, though. The reality of the situation was hitting me hard. Although I'd fought for so long to be considered a warrior, now I had no choice.

Maybe I was weird, but for me, that changed things.

The last of the wolves left before sunset, leaving only a few Guards behind to travel with my parents and Faelen as their protective detail. Saleem and Scarlet left as well, saying they needed to return to the Black Souls Market to prepare for the coming battle. Many of their friends had died. I vowed the Queen was going to pay for that.

Jackson tried not to cry when he'd learned he'd be leaving with Connor and not staying behind with our mother and father to see me off tomorrow morning. I almost cried myself when he told me he'd try to be as brave as I was.

If only he knew how terrified I really was, how much I wished I could run away from this. And that feeling was odd in itself. I'd never felt the urge to run away from anything before, but I panicked every time I thought of fighting the ancient vampire. My parents, Faelen, Skye, and Cyrus all believed I could kill the Queen, but deep down, I wasn't sure I'd be able to pull it off.

The Vampire Queen had been alive and wielding power for centuries. How was I—a young, untried wolf—supposed to kill her, even with my newfound power? Power I had yet to learn how to control, I might add. It didn't look good.

Where are you, Will?

I made my way through the forest just as twilight turned to night.

We need to talk!

He said he'd follow me anywhere. But if I left tomorrow without seeing him, I wasn't sure how long it'd take for him to find me again. Or if he'd even be able to.

Levi had told Darian—and only Darian—where to take me before he left, so wherever we were going, I had a feeling it wouldn't be easy for anyone to follow us—including Will.

I stopped walking and placed a hand against a nearby tree. Looking up, I could see twinkling stars scattered in the dark night sky, and I recalled the Goddess's skin.

"You said you'd lend me power when I need it, adding to what I already have. I really hope you meant that, because I'm going to need it."

A scent I hadn't smelled in far too long hit my nostrils, and I closed my eyes and sighed. My heart was racing as I turned slowly and came face-to-face with red eyes. They soon faded to an ocean blue, and Will removed the hood hiding his face.

We stared at each other for a moment, the air sizzling between us. I wanted to run to him, to feel his arms wrapped around me, but my doubts held me back. As much as I wanted to be with him, I couldn't help remembering that he might not be everything I thought he was.

"I'm sorry I was away for so long." He stepped towards me, and I swallowed hard. My mouth was dry as he reached up and pinched my chin, tilting my head back. His fingers were burning into my skin and he frowned, no doubt hearing my galloping heartbeat. "Are you okay? What's wrong?" He began looking me up and down with concern, and I shook my head.

"Nothing. I'm fine. Did you learn anything?"

His hand fell away from my chin, and he stepped back. His eyes were still roaming my face with concern. Because of the high level of anxiety I was feeling, my wolf stirred, and my skin tingled with impending change. But I couldn't lose control right now. So instead, I stepped forward and took his hand in mine.

"Please, tell me the truth. Did you learn anything?"

"Yes," he answered, his jaws clenched. "My mother is the one behind the disappearances."

I released his hand and allowed mine to fall to my side.

He wasn't looking at me anymore. "But why do I feel like you already knew that, Elinor?"

"What makes you say that?"

He didn't answer immediately, but his eyes found mine and remained there. "I'm very old, Elinor, and after living as long as I have, it gets easier and easier to read others. You were tricky to read in the beginning. It's one reason I was so drawn to you." He lifted a hand to touch my face but stopped. "But now I know you a little better. And you're not looking at me the way I thought you would after not seeing me for so long. There's broken trust in your eyes." A small smile grew on his lips. "I knew something was wrong the minute you didn't throw yourself at me."

"Because if I don't just automatically throw myself at you, it must mean something's wrong? You could be the one to throw yourself at me every once in a while, you know."

He chuckled. "I would do that right now, but I need to know what's going on before I touch you again. I don't want to lose an arm."

I relaxed a little just from seeing him smile. What was it about this man's smile that always made me feel better, no matter what else was going on in my life?

"Yes, I already knew." I sighed and stepped around him. "Saleem and Scarlet went to the location Arden gave us. A General attacked them. I'm assuming it was one of your brothers?"

I turned to face him and saw a flash of hatred in his eyes. "Yes, that was my brother Cain. This was all his idea, his plan."

"So it wasn't the Queen then?"

"Oh, she's involved. But Cain's the one who pushed for her to do this. They want to reclaim the land that was stolen from them long ago, the land they were forced to flee from. But this time, they intend to take a little more."

I scoffed as a gentle wind caressed my face, and I moved the single braid down my back over my shoulder. "And they're using supernaturals to do it. Clever."

"Yes, but I don't think that's all there is to it. Something else is going on, I'm sure of it. Cain is after something—I'm just not sure what. I don't know if the Queen knows or not. If she does, she doesn't seem to care." He paused. "Cain's not as strong as I am, but he shouldn't be underestimated. What he lacks in strength, he makes up for in intelligence. My—"

He stopped speaking, and I frowned. "What? Tell me."

"Part of the reason my mother is doing this is for me," he answered.

My eyes narrowed. "What do you mean?"

He must have fed before coming to see me because his skin was pale and his heart wasn't beating, so he wasn't breathing. But he inhaled deeply, no doubt an involuntary gesture.

I waited, but he said nothing. "Will?"

He took another deep breath. "The reason she wants to reclaim so much land is so that she can give it to me when she steps down." He shook his head. "She's doing it for me, but I swear to you, Elinor, I had no idea."

He combed his hair back with his fingers. "I don't live at the castle anymore. And I stay as far away from vampire business as possible. That's why they didn't feel the need to tell me what they were doing." A chuckle that held no humor slipped from his lips. "It's funny. I had been happy that they'd seemed to have forgotten about me, but now, I wish that wasn't the case. Maybe I would have been able to stop this before it had even started."

His words made me think of Cyrus. He, too, would be forced to live a life he didn't want. I no longer had that problem—my father had given up on trying to marry me off—but while I was somewhat free of that now, Will and Cyrus were still trapped.

I knew how they felt. I could relate to their pain.

Will moved his cloak over his shoulders, and my eyes drifted to the neckline of his shirt. The thought of what his muscular chest and abs might look like without that shirt distracted me for a moment. When my eyes returned to his face, he shook his head.

"Don't look at me like that."

"I was just—"

I swallowed the rest of my words as he cupped my cheeks with both hands and kissed me. I sagged against his body, and he snaked his hands around me to pick me up. My legs dangled off the ground as I moaned into his mouth.

His body was so cold compared to mine, but the contrast felt soothing to me. He gently placed me back on my feet, his lips gliding across mine before he tipped my head back and kissed my throat.

My body stiffened, but not with fear. His fingers moved to my hair, and my eyes fluttered closed as his lips traveled slowly, leaving a trail of hot kisses to my ear.

"You thought I had betrayed you, didn't you?" he whispered, his cool breath causing goosebumps to dot my flesh.

"Um, only a little," I answered and then gasped as he gently nipped the top of my ear.

"Why? I will never betray you, Little Wolf. Never. What will it take for you to finally trust me?" He pulled away and stared down at me, his fingers still tangled in my hair.

I reached up to trace the outline of his lips. "I'm sorry. I do trust you, I just didn't know what to think. But, Will, you know what has to happen, right? The Queen will have to pay for what she's done."

"I know," he answered, suddenly serious. He released my hair but kept a firm hand on my waist. "I may not have betrayed you, but I have betrayed her. She's still my mother, and for that, I feel . . . torn. But I won't side with her on this. I'm not blind to the fact that my mother and my kind are poisonous."

"Then will you help us end this? Will you show us how to get to the castle?"

His hand fell away from my waist, and my heart broke because I could see that his heart was hurting, too. No matter the state of their relationship now, there was a time when he'd ruled by his mother's side. The thought of betraying her must be eating him alive.

I looked away, because I realized that when this was all over, I, too, would hurt my family by leaving the pack and going with Will. My family, and especially my father, would never understand.

"I'll help you," he finally answered, his eyes hard. "The world my mother and brother are creating isn't one I want to live in. After I discovered the truth, I decided I would do everything I could to stop them—with or without help."

"I knew you would help," I replied. "But there's more. We learned something else about the Queen. She's Cyrus's great-grand-niece many times over."

Will's eyes slid to the side contemplatively. "Of course." He frowned. "I hadn't even thought of that. She was a by-product of his father raping a goddess."

"The Demon King raped a goddess? Hell, I already thought he was bad enough from the way Cyrus described him, but if he raped a goddess, he's way worse than I thought."

"Yes, but let's not get into that. I should have thought about . . ." He paused, his eyes widening, and he looked me up and down. "How are you planning to defeat her?"

"How were you?" I shot back, and his eyes narrowed.

"No," he replied, his voice murderous. "I won't let you do it. Why didn't I think of this?" He turned his back to me and walked away. "You're a white wolf. Wolves like you existed before my time, and you've proven the rumors to be true. You have divinity enough to face her. But you can't do it. I won't let you."

"I don't have a choice, and you can't stop me."

"The fuck I can't!"

I stepped back as his loud words echoed through the forest.

He blinked rapidly. "I'm sorry, but you're not ready to face my mother, Elinor. I'm not saying that to belittle your strength. But I know how powerful my mother is. You just recently gained your new power, and you're still not in control of it. My mother has been wielding her power for centuries."

"Then how were you going to stop her?" He grew silent, and I crossed my arms over my chest as I waited. "Well?"

"I can easily handle my brother. And while I can't kill my mother, I can weaken her enough that she can be trapped."

I shrugged. "You still didn't tell me what your plan was."

"My venom is toxic to vampires." He pinched the bridge of his nose. "It's something only older vampires know, ones that were alive centuries ago when I was a different man. My mother commanded them never to speak of it, so the younger vampires, the ones who now hate me, would never know."

"I get it. It would give them more reason to say you're some kind of freak," I said, and he nodded.

"Yes. A vampire's venom is toxic and potent to other species but does nothing when used on each other. Except for mine. I can't kill the Queen, but I can wound her enough for us to contain her."

Containing her wasn't going to be enough to make up for all the things she'd done. I was confident that every species would agree on that, but Will might have just given me a great idea.

"Then we have the perfect plan, Will. Don't you see? Between you, me, and Cyrus, we can defeat her."

Even though he said he was on our side, I figured it was better not to keep talking about killing her. I knew, deep down, he understood what I was saying. But I also understood what this was costing him.

I stepped forward and took his hands into mine.

All the doubt I had previously felt evaporated, and confidence filled me. "We can do this. Cyrus is powerful, and he would have been by my side to begin with. But with your power added, I know we can do this. I can do this."

As terrified as I was, I had to do my part, even if it killed me. And for a while there, I thought it would. But now, with Will helping us, I couldn't help feeling like we actually stood a chance of defeating her.

"Okay," he answered, reluctantly nodding.

"I forgot to tell you . . . I'm leaving tomorrow morning, and you can't follow me," I blurted out, covering his mouth with my hand before he could protest. "I have to—orders from the Council. They want me to go into hiding so I can learn to control these new powers." I dropped my hand from his mouth. "How long do you think it'll take for your mother to find out who and what I am?"

He pulled me against him. "Unfortunately, she probably already knows. So going into hiding isn't a bad idea. And learning to control those powers is definitely a good thing. But me not following you?" He laughed. "That's not going to happen."

"Will . . ."

"I'll keep my distance, but I'm not letting you out of my sight. If we're going to do this together, I need to stay close."

I thought about that for a moment, and I had to admit, he was right. "Okay."

We fell silent, and he moved a strand of my hair behind my ear. "We make a pretty good team, don't we?"

My cheeks heated. "It would seem so."

We did indeed make a great team, and I pressed my lips together as a new sensation warmed the pit of my stomach. I felt terrible that I had harbored doubts about Will. But with the way he was looking at me now with such raw love in his gaze, those thoughts were silenced. He leaned forward and placed his forehead against mine. It was such a simple action, but it held so much meaning.

"I love you," I breathed out, the words slipping from my lips of their own accord.

He kissed my forehead. "I love you, too."

His lips claimed mine, and my eyes fluttered closed as he pulled my bottom lip into his mouth. He sucked on it gently, once, twice, and then released it, and I fisted his shirt.

My breathing became shallow as his hands snaked around me to rest on my hips. He stepped forward, closing the space between us, and I mentally urged his hand to slide lower.

I'd never been attracted to anyone the way I was to Will, so I'd never wanted to get intimate with anyone before. But ever since I'd met Will, I'd lain awake countless nights, my body yearning for his touch. And now, as I stared up into his blue eyes that were slowly turning red, I knew I was truly ready to share everything with him, body and soul.

Who knew what the future held for us? We could talk and plan as much as we wanted, but nothing was guaranteed.

And I don't want to die without ever feeling William's body against mine.

I frowned at that thought. I couldn't think like that. I wasn't going to die. But I didn't want to ignore what I wanted any longer, either. I wanted Will with every fiber of my being, and I knew that would never change.

He took a deep breath, and a crease appeared between his brows. "Your scent, Elinor. You're . . . I can smell your—" He swallowed hard. "—your arousal. You don't know what you're doing to me. I need you to calm down."

My cheeks were burning as I looked down, unable to face him right now. "And what if I don't want to?"

His hand slid further down my body, and I gasped as he gently grabbed and squeezed my bottom, pulling my body tight up against him so I could feel the evidence of his excitement.

"Then I need you to say it. Tell me what you want, Elinor."

I swallowed hard and held his stare. My lips parted, but I

couldn't speak—couldn't bring myself to say the words I wanted to—that I wanted him. My teeth sank into my lower lip as he suddenly lifted me off the ground. I gripped his shoulder and wrapped my legs around his waist.

"I need to hear the words, Elinor. Say them."

"I-I want you . . . I want you to be my first."

This time when he kissed me, he wasn't gentle. But I didn't mind it, and I matched his urgency with my own fire. Unwrapping my legs from around him, he shifted my weight so that he was carrying me like he would a bride.

The trees around us blurred as he sprinted through the forest, and I clung to him. I didn't know where he was taking me, but I would gladly go anywhere with him. I trusted this man with my life, and I knew I wasn't foolish to do so.

He ran for a few minutes, then stopped and placed me on my feet in front of an abandoned house. Because the place didn't look as battered and decrepit as I would have thought they'd be, I looked at Will questioningly.

"I come here sometimes," he admitted, taking my hand and leading me inside. "When I need space."

I was surprised to find the place clean, though rather empty. "This is awfully close to my pack. Weren't you ever worried about being discovered?"

He didn't answer as he gently tugged on my hand, and I followed him towards a closed door. When he opened it, my heart skipped a beat when I saw the lightly furnished bedroom.

I swallowed hard, the sound audible, and Will paused and turned to me. He smiled knowingly, and my cheeks flushed. It only worsened my embarrassment. "If you wish, Elinor, we can just lay here for a while together. I've constantly thought about simply lying next to you. I'd be satisfied with that, if it's what you want."

I sighed. Will was so extraordinary in every way. Yes, I'd

imagined the same thing that he had, but I'd wished for so much more, and I was tired of waiting. Without thinking, I rose on my tiptoes and kissed him. For a moment, I lost myself in the feel of him and the way his cool lips felt on mine before I pulled away.

I poured my need into my eyes because I knew I couldn't voice the words.

He reached out for me and gripped my waist firmly, but not painfully, and kissed my cheeks, my forehead, and then my ears and neck. All the while, his hands were dragging my shirt out from my pants.

He was being so gentle, going so slow—it was agonizing. The anticipation was eating me up inside. I could tell by the strained look on his face that he was doing his best to hold back. But he wasn't finding it easy to do.

"I won't break," I told him, and he paused. "You don't have to hold back. I'm not that fragile."

His fangs descended, and his eyes darted to my neck. "I'm not worried about breaking you. But from that first moment, I wanted to consume you—all of you. I craved your blood, and . . . I still do. If I lose control now . . . I just don't want to hurt you."

"What is it like?" I asked, and he closed his eyes. "What does the craving feel like?"

He stepped away from me and sat down on the bed. "It's like being thirsty while in chains, and there is a goblet of water just before you." He licked his lips and looked up at me from under his lashes. "You feel like you'll rip the world apart just to have a single drop of it, but you know if you break free from the chains, you'll lose control and waste it all. You'll attack the goblet and spill most of what you had just been craving."

His eyes rolled down my body, and even though I was still fully clothed, I felt naked. It was almost as if he was touching me with his eyes, and maybe I was crazy, but I wanted him to feed on me. I wanted to give myself to him in every way.

"That's what wanting you feels like. I'm afraid I might rip you apart."

I removed my shirt with shaky hands, and his jaw clenched so hard, I feared his teeth would shatter. After a few minutes, I was down to only my undergarments, and I shivered as he gripped the edges of the bed. I don't know what it was—maybe simply the fact that he craved me so much, or perhaps it was just the love and pain in his eyes—but suddenly, I felt so brave.

"Elinor . . ." he drawled, and I stepped forward.

"I'm not afraid." I began pulling my braid out and allowed my slightly curled hair to fall over my shoulder. "You'll stop. I know you will."

It took a moment to truly convince him I wanted this, but he soon laid down beside me and caressed me lightly with his fingers.

"Will it hurt?" I asked through barely parted lips.

He shook his head, his eyes on my exposed throat. "You'll feel a small prick, but I'll make it pleasurable. I promise you that."

I nodded and moved to adjust myself beside him, but his hand moved so swiftly, pinning me down, that I froze.

"Don't move."

I didn't nod or speak as my pulse hammered away in my ear. I closed my eyes, and he moved closer to me, his thumb on my side gently caressing my skin. I tried to contain myself as he kissed my shoulder, and my body slowly arched as he slid his hand from my side to under my back. He buried his face in my neck, and my breath hitched as his cool tongue swiped against my skin.

My father would definitely have a stroke if he caught us at this very moment.

Are you serious? Don't think about your father right now!

"Now is the time to change your mind, Little Wolf."

I realized then that my eyes had been closed the whole time, but as I opened them, my heartbeat skyrocketed at the sight of him. His cheek was next to mine, but I could see his transformed self's pale skin and the black veins covering his cheek. He leaned up a little.

"Do it," I told him, and a strangled cry fell from my lips as his fangs pierced my skin.

The pain was sharp and rippled across my neck, but as he had promised, it only lasted a second. My tense body relaxed as he started sucking, and I could feel my blood rushing to the surface of my skin. It was an odd sensation, yet a thrilling one. The only thing that mattered to me was the feeling of having his fangs buried in my flesh. I wrapped my hands around his neck as he settled his body between my legs.

Everything I'd ever imagined didn't compare to this. A feeling of complete and utter bliss consumed me as his hold on me tightened. My canines and claws sprouted, a sure sign that I was feeling something extraordinary. As he pulled away to take a deep breath, a line of blood ran down the sides of his mouth.

We both froze as a drop of blood fell from his chin onto my face.

I smiled, and then we both started laughing. My body felt a little weak, but it was more from ecstasy and not from the loss of blood.

"Sorry." He wiped a finger across my cheek. "Are you okay?"

I blinked slowly. I felt a little drunk but fabulous. I reached up and moved my hair from my other shoulder. "Please," I pleaded softly. "Do it again, but this time I want more. I want all of you."

18

ELINOR

*M*y eyes were closed, but I was wide awake. I'd felt sore before after hours of training, but never in such an intimate place. I welcomed the feeling, the slight ache, a reminder of something I would never forget.

Images of what Will and I had done a few hours ago filled my mind, and for the first time since the world started to fall apart, I felt happy.

I pushed away all thoughts of what was yet to come. I only focused on the here and now and how Will had wiped out any lingering doubts I'd had of how he felt about me. I was more motivated to move forward now that I'd learned about another one of Will's abilities—one that was fatal to vampires—and that he'd be using it to help us.

I knew this wasn't going to be easy for him—the moment he'd have to betray the Queen, his mother, to her face. But what she was doing was madness, and I was relieved he could see that. She wanted to expand her domain, but starting a war wasn't the way to do it. The world had moved past barbarity, for the most part. Species no longer had to fight over territories. We came together and made agreements that worked for everyone. Of course, there were still ongoing feuds and a fair amount of racism between some species. But nothing big enough to start a war.

I couldn't help wondering, however, what was going to happen once the Queen was dead. Would all the vampires die, and if not, would they elect another queen or king, allowing the cycle of bloodshed to continue? Had Will thought about that? His kind already disliked him. Upon finding out what he'd done, would they all try to kill him?

Or would they be too afraid to face the man who'd defeated the Queen?

One thing at a time.

First, we needed to be rid of the Queen, and then we could worry about what came next.

Will's body, now warm after feeding, moved beside me, and the bed beneath us dipped, but I kept my eyes closed. He moved on top of me, and I tried to stifle the blush creeping onto my face.

I opened my eyes, and my blush quickly faded as I tried to make sense of what I saw. "Will, what are you doing?"

Above me, Will was in his vampire form, the sharp blade of a knife in his hand coming rapidly towards my face. I reacted, pushing against his chest, and he flew off me and landed across the room.

He sprang to his feet within seconds, his fangs on display as he hissed loudly. I rolled off the bed, my fangs elongating out of reflex. I was as naked as he was, but I didn't care about that. What concerned me was that I didn't know who I was looking at. Will's eyes were filled with rage and murder, his skin covered in black veins.

"Will, what the hell are you doing? What's going on?"

My body was shaking, my thoughts rolling over each other in a jumbled mess as I tried to make sense of what was happening. Will stood up straight from being hunched forward and his hand with the knife lowered. His eyes were bright red flames, redder and more murderous than I had ever seen them. And for the first time since meeting him, I felt afraid.

A chill went down my spine as his tongue glided over his fangs. "Will?"

He vanished out of sight, and I moved immediately, heading for the door. But he appeared right in front of me, slamming into me, causing us both to fall. We rolled on the ground, and a howl of pain escaped me as I felt his claws pierce my side.

I punched his face, the sound of his nose breaking echoing inside the empty room, and it sent him hurtling backward yet again. I knew if I stayed, he'd kill me.

Pain like nothing I'd ever felt before bloomed inside my heart and began spreading across my chest as I ran out the door.

"Run, Little Wolf! Run!"

I was wrong about him—so wrong!

Tears blurred my vision as Will's snarl echoed through the night, and I continued running through the forest, twigs grabbing at my exposed skin. I ignored the healing sensation of the wound on my side and pushed forward.

I could hear him chasing me, gaining on me quickly. When I tried to tap into my power, it was silent within me, and I cursed under my breath. I doubted any Guards were this deep in the forest, especially off our territory. No one would hear me if I howled for help.

Why? Why is he doing this? What the hell is going on?

"Elinor!" Will's enraged cry broke the last piece of my heart that hadn't yet shattered.

I didn't know the man behind me. His eyes had none of the warmth that I'd become accustomed to. I had given so much of myself to him—all of me, really. But everything I'd received in return had been a lie. As my side healed, the blood yet to dry still running down my thigh, I knew I had to face reality.

My mind was still a tangled mess of wanting to understand what had gone wrong, but I wouldn't get answers from him. Faelen had been right about Will. So had Cyrus. I'd foolishly put myself in a situation where I might die. And I deserved it.

Wiping at a tear, I wondered for a moment if I should shift. But if I did so, I'd have to slow down, and he'd catch up to me. I could already hear him on my heels. Now the soreness I had felt before wasn't bringing me joy. I felt disgusted. I felt sick in every sense of the word, and I barely winced as I ran past some bushes and a twig slashed my thigh.

I could feel blood trickling down my thigh, but I kept running. I poured my energy into my legs to propel me forward. The physical pain was nothing compared to the emotional one that was slowing me down.

I clenched my fists, a feeling of relief filling me as the border to my pack's territory came into view. I wouldn't be safe when I crossed over, but the second I did, a howl like no one had ever heard before would leave my lips. And I would no longer be alone.

I'll never forgive him for this!

I closed my eyes for a second because I knew that was a lie. Even now, running for my life, my mind was replaying all the moments we had spent together—the time we'd first met, and the many circumstances when he'd saved my life. My chest tightened, just thinking of the way he had looked at me mere hours ago as I gave myself to him.

I loved him—I truly loved him! How could he do this to me?

Without warning, Will tackled me to the ground, and we rolled for a few seconds, clawing and biting at each other before we came to a stop with him on top of me.

"Get off me! Get the fuck off me! How could you?"

"How could I? You're pathetic!" Will laughed, and I screamed as his nails pierced my right upper arm, pinning me to the forest floor. "You thought you could kill the Queen? You!"

I made the mistake of looking into his eyes. As I lifted my left hand to hit him, he spoke. "Stop."

My hand froze mid-air.

He adjusted himself so he was straddling me, his weight bearing down on me. "Lower your hand."

My hand fell lifelessly. He was compelling me, an ability I had forgotten he possessed. Hot tears streamed down my cheeks, though I tried to stop them. I didn't want to cry. I didn't want to give him the satisfaction, but I couldn't help myself.

Above me sat William, son of the Vampire Queen—future Vampire King. The Will I thought I had known was gone.

I snarled and snapped my jaw at him, but he only laughed in response, a sinister sound. His eyes traveled up and down my body before he moved his right hand from behind him, brandishing a knife, and my heart skipped a beat.

"You don't have to do this," I pleaded.

"But I do." He tilted his head and his ruffled hair fell to the side. "Don't speak, Little Wolf. As much as I'd love to hear you scream, I can't have you alerting your pack."

I tried to open my mouth but couldn't. My body was entirely under his control, and I closed my eyes as he cupped one of my breasts.

"You really are beautiful, I'll give you that. Such a waste. You would have made a powerful vampire if turned."

I hate you! I hate you so much!

I wanted to scream those words at him. I wanted to rip him limb from limb. The fact that I couldn't, coupled with my throbbing broken heart, was only fueling my wrath.

More than anything, I wanted to forget everything, to sink into the ground and cease to exist. I was a fool! A fool to have ever loved this monster!

I opened my eyes, but I shouldn't have. I just laid there and watched as the knife's blade pierced my chest and heart.

I sat up, gasping for air. Will was shaking me violently. I swiped my claws across his chest, but he moved back just in time to avoid a deep wound.

"Elinor, wake up!"

I paused, my breath hitching as I stared wide-eyed around the room. I was back in the small bedroom with Will, his chest wound slowly healing. I looked down at my naked chest, expecting to see a knife embedded there, but there was nothing. Then I looked up and saw Will looking at me with a mixture of panic and anger.

"I-I'm so sorry," I stuttered. "I was dreaming."

"I know," he said, hastily putting his clothes back on.

I held my head as it throbbed. It had all been a dream. I placed my hand over my heart and began taking deep breaths to calm myself. I looked over at him. "Will, your chest. I'm so sorry."

"It wasn't your fault. We need to go right now." He picked up his shirt off the ground. "Fuck!"

I slid off the bed, now confused by how upset he was. "What's going on?"

He pulled his pants up and buttoned them before answering. "What did you see?"

I frowned but told him all about the terrible dream. It had felt so real, and when I touched my cheek, I found it wet with tears.

Will pulled his shirt over his head. "I just had a nightmare as well. That can only mean one thing. My brother Cain is close."

That's not good.

I bent down to collect my clothes that were strewn around the room.

"What does my nightmare have to do with your brother? And what do you mean, he's coming? Did he cause both of us to have nightmares?"

"Yes and no," Will answered. "My brother's power is the ability to control others' fear. He can make that fear appear to you whether you're awake or asleep. The closer he is to you, the stronger it affects you. Your fear paralyzes you, making it easy for him to kill you in the end." Then his eyes grew sad. "But he only makes you see what you already fear. He can't control what you see."

Neither of us said anything for a moment. Then he walked over to me to cup my cheek. "You fear being betrayed by me, but you have no reason to, Elinor. I love you, and that will never change."

"I love you, too," I whispered back, but my heart still felt shattered from the dream. "It-it felt so real, Will. I thought you . . ."

He closed his eyes and sighed. "I know."

"Okay, so then this means your mother knows about me?"

"I think it's safe to assume that's the reason Cain's here," he answered as he adjusted his cloak to cover his body. "My mother must have sent him to kill you. But I won't let that happen."

I grabbed his arm as he began walking towards the door. "What are you going to do? You can't stop him. If you do, they'll know you're on our side. If your mother has learned about me, we've already lost one element of surprise. We can't lose another."

He ran a hand down his face, and I grew even more anxious, sensing his unease. I could almost see the wheels turning inside his head as his eyes darted back and forth.

"I have to. I'll distract him while you get back to your

pack. You all have to leave immediately. Because if he gets there . . ." His words trailed off, and I swallowed hard. "Paranoia goes hand-in-hand with fear. He can make you all kill each other."

He pulled a bottle out of his pocket and drank its contents, and within seconds, I could no longer smell his scent. Everything was moving too quickly for me. This wasn't how I had imagined we'd part ways after what we'd shared a few hours ago.

He kissed my forehead, then my lips, and turned away, but I tightened my hold on his hand.

"What did you see?"

His jaw visibly clenched, and his eyes turned red. I knew he was trying to hide his emotions from me, but he was more rattled than I'd ever seen him. Will was always calm and collected, his voice rarely rising in pitch. But right now, he was unnerved, and that told me that his brother was a threat to all of us.

Well, he's a General, Elinor.

"You need to go." He pulled the hood of his cloak over his head. "You need to go now."

Elinor

My nails dug into the earth as I ran back to the pack house, and this time, when I called on my power to enhance my speed, it worked. Saying I was relieved was an understatement. I was still shaken by that dream but did my best to not focus on it.

Summoning my power like this was easy, but controlling the electricity I could feel simmering beneath my flesh was another matter. If Cain, as Will had called him, caught up to us and successfully turned me against my family, I wasn't sure anyone would survive.

I shifted back into my human form when I got closer to my house, which was quiet, except for a few muffled voices. I rushed inside and found my father, Cyrus, and Darian in the living room.

When he saw me, my father got to his feet. "Elinor? What's wrong?"

"They're coming, he's coming, a vampire General's coming. And we need to leave tonight!"

"What are you talking about?" Cyrus asked, and I pinched the bridge of my nose.

I was still charged with adrenaline, so I took a few deep breaths. "The Queen knows about me, and a vampire General's on his way to the pack right now to kill me. We can't wait until tomorrow to leave. We have to go tonight."

Darian's hazel eyes narrowed accusingly. "How do you know this?"

"That's not important right now. If we stay here, we will die."

My mother, Faelen, and Skye entered the living room. Their eyes darted from person to person as they sensed the tension.

Needing an outlet for my adrenaline, I paced and forth in front of the couch. "The General can control fear—he'll make us kill each other. I have no doubt he's the General that Saleem and Scarlet faced."

"How do you know all of this, Elinor? Where have you been?" My father was slipping into his overprotective mode, but now wasn't the time for that.

Every second mattered—we'd already lost our element of surprise against the Queen. At least one of them. But now wasn't the time to tell anyone about Will and the plan we came up with.

"We can ask questions later." Faelen stepped forward. "Do you know how long we have before he gets here, Elinor?"

I stopped in front of her and shook my head. "I'm not sure. Less than an hour, maybe."

"That's not enough time," Skye muttered to herself.

My mother stepped forward to move a strand of my hair behind my ear. "It'll have to be enough." But she was looking at me strangely, as if she was searching for something, and I became self-conscious.

My father was looking at me suspiciously as well, and I knew he was thinking about Will. He looked at Darian, and I sensed a silent conversation happening between them. As much as I was curious about what they were thinking, there was no time to ponder. We had already packed our bags with supplies and could leave immediately.

"I'm going with Elinor," Cyrus announced.

Darian bobbed his head. "I already knew you'd want to come. That's fine."

My father began walking towards the door. "Gather everything, everyone, but we won't separate here. We have to travel together so I can see to it that Elinor gets far enough away."

"No." I made a face. "There's no need for that, Father."

"I'm not leaving you," he argued.

I sighed exasperatedly. "Father, Cyrus and Darian will be with me. You need to stay with Mother and Faelen. I doubt the General came alone. You have to protect Mother and Faelen."

"And you need to get back to the pack as soon as possi-ble," Darian added. "They need you with them. I can take care of Elinor."

My father looked at me, then Darian, then Skye, and finally Cyrus. There was a bulging vein on his forehead, and the tips of his ears turned red. My mother stepped forward and placed her hand on his shoulder. They gazed at each other for a moment, and then he exhaled.

"Protect her," he growled at Darian. "Be safe, all of you. How will I know you've gotten to wherever you're going safely?"

"I'll mind-link with Darian once we get to the pack," Faelen confirmed.

While my father still looked hesitant about this course of action, he finally conceded.

My mother pulled me into a tight embrace. "Remember what I told you. I'm proud of you. End this and come back to me. I want my daughter back."

I nodded, and Faelen placed a hand on my shoulder and squeezed tightly. Even though I didn't always appreciate it when she spoke her mind, I knew she meant well. And we had a mutual enemy: Levi. What was that saying? The enemy of my enemy was my friend?

I placed my hand over hers. "Thank you."

She smiled, and the skin under her eyes crinkled. Then she left the room with everyone except my father. He still looked displeased about the plan to split up, but there was no choice. I was the one Cain was after. And I wouldn't be alone —I'd have Cyrus, Darian, and Skye with me.

Plus, I wasn't anywhere near defenseless, myself. Hopefully, whatever Will was planning to do would work, and he'd delay Cain long enough for us to get far enough away that we couldn't be followed.

"You have to let me go, Father."

He released a long breath. "I'm trying to." He pressed a finger to the crease between his brows. "But you don't make it easy."

"What's that supposed to mean?"

"You were with the vampire, weren't you?"

"Yes," I answered after a moment, and he turned away. "I was, and he can be trusted."

"Until he can't be," he argued.

I sighed. "Just like you can only trust Cyrus until he can't be trusted? Are you waiting for that day?"

He turned to face me. "Cyrus is different."

"He's a dark creature, like Will. He's the son of the Demon King and a Sin. Believe me, he's more like Will than you know."

Now was not the time for us to have this argument. I was more than willing to defend Will, but if my father and I started this conversation and if I said too much, this situation would only go downhill. I'd have to tell him about Will eventually to explain the plan he and I had come up with, but I'd have to be careful not to share the romantic aspect of things.

Maybe my father had already figured out that part, though. I could see he was fighting his fatherly instinct to protect and his wolf's instinct to reject others outside of the pack. Not that my father had ever made decisions solely based on his wolf's instincts. This was the same Alpha who'd saved and welcomed a young demon into our pack.

Will had fought by my side, protected Jackson, warned us about the upcoming danger, and was helping us to get away.

My father had always been more than just an Alpha who cared for his people. He was also a compassionate one who tried his best to be fair and nonjudgmental. He had good intentions, but even the best of intentions could yield bad decisions if he let his protective instincts get in the way of his better judgment. His past attempts to control my life were perfect examples of that. But the way he was with Cyrus showed that he was capable of seeing past race and focusing on who a person was at their core.

"He can help us kill her, Father. He has a power that'll

weaken her. Between Will, Cyrus, and me, we can finish her. I need you to trust me on that."

He took me by the shoulders gently. "Then enough secrets. If you want me to trust you, tell me who he is."

I stared up at him. We were parting ways tonight, and I wasn't sure when I'd see him again. So I told him who Will was, and the part he'd played in saving Skye. I told him about that night in the forest, when he had saved me from two Bleeders. And then I told him Will's secret.

His hands dropped from my shoulders.

I understood. A vampire who could walk in the sun, who had a soul, was a lot to take in. But he kept listening and didn't say a word to interrupt.

I explained about Will's poisonous venom next, and that he was willing to help, but, of course, I omitted what we did in the little cottage in the woods. When I was finished speaking, we just stared at each other for a long time. I didn't say it, but I was sure he could tell that Will was much more than a friend to me.

He looked wounded, angry even, and a little confused, but he contained it all and remained silent.

"Father?"

"I'm processing," he grumbled. Then he covered his mouth with his left hand and sighed, looking thoughtful.

I allowed him the time to mull over it all. It generally took me a while to process things, and he only had a couple minutes before we had to leave.

"He'll follow you and Darian, then," he said, and I nodded. "Darian won't understand—well, he will, but he won't like it. It took him a long time to accept Cyrus."

"I know. But he doesn't have any choice in the matter. It's up to me to kill the Queen, and I'll need Cyrus and Will to do it."

"Goddess," my father exhaled heavily. "A vampire who can walk in the sun. How is that even possible?"

"I don't know, but it is." I stepped forward and snaked my hand around him. He froze for a moment, shocked that I was hugging him, then his arms wrapped around me. "You took that better than I expected."

"That's only because I'm thinking about the bigger picture —killing the Queen. But if it turns out that he's anything like her, we'll have a bigger problem on our hands." He pulled back. "You know what we'll have to do if that happens, right? You know what'll happen when the Council finds out about him? They might allow him to fight with us now, but when this is over, they'll target him next."

I nodded. "Yes, I know."

But he and I will be long gone by then. Because when this is all over, they'll be after me, too.

"We need to go." We both turned and found Cyrus at the door. My father nodded to him, and Cyrus did the same. "Elinor, we'll be outside."

Cyrus turned and left, and my father's large hand came down on my shoulder. He didn't say anything, and I was happy he didn't. I didn't want us to say goodbye like we'd never see each other again.

I placed my hand over my heart as he did the same, and we bowed at the same time. And at that moment, I understood that I'd finally gained my father's respect and trust.

19

WILL

*T*he world around me blurred as I raced through the woods. While werewolves were agile creatures, vampires were still miles ahead of them in the speed department. Vampires, as natural predators, were stealthier. However, with their strength, final form, and extraordinary senses, werewolves still had no trouble hunting us.

I locked onto my brother's scent and swung left to head in his direction. Cain's ability allowed him to affect supernaturals and humans within a mile of him. My brother enjoyed making people psychically live their worst fear, and he used his gift every chance he got.

But when he directed his attention on one person, the effects were much worse.

As I ran, I sensed his power attempting to pierce my mind. I'd discovered long ago, back when we were both quite young, that the trick to fighting him was to build a wall, a mental barrier, around my thoughts. And though he'd tried long and hard over the years to break through it, he'd never succeeded . . . until now.

I hadn't thought it possible for me to fall victim to his

power. My fists clenched at that, recalling Vivian's words that I was growing weaker. But I knew that wasn't true. I had, however, dropped my guard, and couldn't let that happen again. I swallowed, a lingering taste of Elinor still on my tongue. It had been worth it.

I stopped running when I smelled my brother and his Bleeders. I knew he wouldn't have come alone. By my estimation, he had sixteen others with him, Bleeders and supernaturals alike. To other supernaturals, vampires all smelled the same. But vampires could detect minute differences in each others' scents that made it possible for us to identify specific individuals.

I began walking to the location my brother's scent was strongest, but my mind couldn't help going back to the moment I had bitten Elinor. My gums ached and my fangs elongated at the memory of her exquisite taste and the way she had clung to me. Maybe it was the divinity coursing through her body, but I'd actually lost myself in her taste. For a second, I wasn't sure I'd be able to stop. I'd wanted to consume her. But as soon as she spoke, I realized what I was doing. She wasn't aware of the control she had over me, but at that moment, I'd been glad of it.

I was a little surprised at how quickly she'd broken through to me, her words easily pulling me back from the ledge that I'd worked to hold myself back from for centuries.

Elinor had given herself to me without fear. She'd never truly understand how much that meant to me.

For so long, I'd felt alone and unwanted. I thought I had been cursed to walk the earth by myself, feared or hated—never loved. For a while I'd deceived myself into believing my mother loved me, but now I knew that she hadn't, not really. Unfortunately, it had taken centuries for me to realize that. I was just her most incredible creation. She was both proud of what she created and fascinated by the potential of what I represented.

I didn't want to pass on my ability to walk during the day, and not because I was trying to keep it all to myself. Even without the ability to daywalk, vampires were already capable of mass destruction—a destruction I'd already played a major part in. If vampires could walk in the sun too . . . If every vampire had my ability, they would overrun the world within weeks. And I couldn't let that happen.

Hopefully, Elinor had already made it back to her pack, and they had left. I found Cain with a Bleeder, the hairless creature crouched down at his side. He turned to face me and waved his hand at the Bleeder, who rushed into the bushes and vanished. He buried his hands in his pockets and glared at me.

"Were you trying to sneak up on me, Will?"

"What are you doing here?" I inquired bluntly, and the corners of his mouth arched.

"I should ask you that," he countered.

"Vivian's coven is close by. That was the reason I was sent here months ago."

He pulled a hand from his pocket and snapped his fingers. "Oh, right. Good luck with that one. She's crazy."

"If you're here for the white wolf, Cain, she's gone, and so is the rest of her pack."

The smug smirk on his face vanished. "And why would you go looking for her?"

"Since neither you nor the Queen would fill me in on what's happening, I found out for myself." I shook my head. "The girl's a white wolf. And I know, the same as you do, what that means to our mother. That's why you're here, right? To kill her?"

He didn't answer right away, but I figured he'd be tight-lipped. Cain was the overly suspicious type, and I doubted he even trusted our mother, though he had glued himself to her side as if he were a toddler.

"They've all already left, so you're too late," I told him. "If I had been advised about all of this beforehand, she wouldn't have slipped through the Queen's hands. So go back and report that to our mother."

Cain's eyes hardened for a moment, and I could see the intended purpose of my words had hit home. There was nothing Cain hated more than failure. Well, he hated me more, but I didn't care about that. I was only trying to stall him. Unfortunately, though he was here, he had sent Bleeders ahead.

But Elinor and her family could easily handle them. My brother was the real threat.

"What happened to you, William?" He spat my name as if it burned his tongue. "I don't mind that you're no longer living at the castle. In fact, I'm quite happy I don't have to see your face. But I'm curious . . . What changed you?"

"Why does that matter, Cain?"

He shrugged, causing a strand of blond hair to graze his face. While I was six foot six and dark, Cain was six foot four and fair. We weren't brothers by blood, so we looked nothing alike. The only thing we had in common in appearance was the fact that we were both muscular.

"I want to understand what happened to you, so I can make sure it doesn't happen to me," he clarified. "You were a legend, and yet, you walked away. What have you been doing while you've roamed the earth like a lost soul?" He smirked. "At least, I'm assuming you have a soul."

"You don't need to concern yourself with my soul, Cain. Worry about our mother's wrath when she finds out you lost the girl."

He hissed. "You were here all this time. Why didn't you capture her?"

"Really? You need to decide what you want me to do—stay out of things or help. Or do you need a few lessons on how to be a General?"

He stepped forward, his fangs long enough to touch his bottom lip, but then stopped. "You know what? It's fine. I have someone following the girl as we speak. It'll only be a matter of time before the Queen has her."

I paused at that. "What do you mean, 'the Queen has her'? Aren't you here to kill her?"

"It's unpleasant not knowing anything, isn't it?" Cain retorted. "That's how I felt before. You were always there, always the one she called on."

"Oh, let it go, Cain. Now you're by her side, and I'm happy you are. So move on."

"So fucking smug!" Cain said as his eyes moved across my face with disgust.

I didn't care. If he was here to capture Elinor instead of kill her, I had to learn why. But I dreaded finding out the answer.

"We don't have time to stand here and bicker like children. I'll help with the search if you tell me what's going on. Why doesn't the Queen want the girl dead? She has strong divinity and is a genuine threat. You know that."

Cain's power suddenly exploded from his body, and I stepped back. I shouldn't have. He noticed the action immediately, and while he frowned with confusion, he quickly smiled knowingly.

"You're affected." He began laughing, the sound rolling up to the trees above. "You have changed! What do you fear, Will? Tell me."

I removed my cloak and flung it to the ground. I felt his power bearing down on me in an attempt to paralyze me, but when he charged at me, I still reacted. It was too late for him to change his course of action, and he dodged my fist by an inch and rolled to the side. He was back on his feet quickly, and we collided, his fangs snapping inches away from my face. My fist grazed his cheek, sending him backwards, but he recovered within seconds and was on me again.

"What do you fear?" he demanded as his fist connected with my gut.

Elinor appeared behind him, her throat slit and tears in her eyes. I swallowed hard as I tried to fortify my mental barriers and stepped back just in time to avoid Cain's claws slicing my throat open. The illusion of Elinor felt so real, I could even smell her.

"Will, help me," she pleaded, her blood spilling over the hand she held to her throat.

Cain looked behind him, a victorious grin on his face. "Oh, I wish I could see what you're seeing. What's changed? My power's never been effective against you before."

I clenched my fists and allowed my claws to pierce my flesh. I needed to remind myself that she wasn't there, and I couldn't allow my fear to distract me, no matter what I saw. Although losing Elinor was my greatest fear, I recognized that she wasn't really hurt. She was long gone by now.

I charged at Cain, and we tumbled to the ground, our mixed snarls and hisses echoing in the dark forest around us. A fight between us had been brewing for centuries, but right now, I needed to do what I had to do in order to uncover his true plan for Elinor.

My fist cracked the earth as Cain moved his head to the side, and when my head swung back, his claws ripped the flesh on my cheek. My heartbeat stopped, and I shifted into my vampire form. When Cain got up, I saw a Bleeder feeding on Elinor by his feet. Her teary eyes were on me, her lips barely parted as she tried to speak. Then she screamed as the Bleeder ripped her throat out, and I grew angry.

I had played around with Cain long enough. "I'm only

going to ask you once more, brother. What does Mother want with her?"

Cain paused. "You know her, don't you?"

"I've been close to this pack for months, so yes, I've seen the girl before. Again, if I had known what was going on, I could have captured her for our mother. But you both decided to keep me in the dark, to your own detriment." I bent my head from side to side, the bones cracking loudly. "Speak, Cain. We don't have all night. And only one of us can track her during the day."

"You aren't my superior, Will. You never have been and you never will be, so don't speak to me as if I am beneath you." Cain was losing his cool, so I remained quiet, waiting for him to answer my question. "I'll take care of the girl."

The silence between us stretched on as I stared at him unblinkingly. His unease grew by the second, and the image of Elinor lying by his feet shimmered. That was what I had been waiting for, for him to be reminded of his place. His strength and power were nothing compared to mine.

Centuries of feuding with Cain surfaced in my mind, and I recalled how he'd secretly sided with the vampires who'd wanted me removed as a General. The man I used to be resurfaced in me, and I saw nothing but a weak vampire who didn't deserve his title. A thirst for blood, for violence, mixed with an intense need to protect the woman I loved blinded me for a second, but that was all it took.

I vanished, the world becoming distorted around me, and reappeared behind Cain. As he was turning around, I grabbed the side of his head and his shoulder, and ignoring the low sound of his bones cracking, I exposed his throat.

Then I bit him, my fangs latching onto his throat. I didn't dull his pain, the way I'd done with Elinor, but of course, it was nothing to him. Then I released him, grabbing his arm as he swung at me. My jaw elongated, and I sank my fangs into his upper arm. I pulled back, tearing his flesh before pushing my hand into his gut. Black blood spewed from his mouth, and I wrapped my arms around him, pinning his body to mine as I bit him again, injecting my venom into his system.

"The Queen will kill you!" He tried to break free from my hold, but I only tightened my arms around him. "I-It's f-forbidden!"

I didn't care that the Queen had forbidden me to use my venom on another vampire. I had already bitten Vivian, and no doubt she'd already run to the Queen. I threw Cain to the ground, and his right hand, with a chunk of flesh missing, immediately went to his neck. The small dose of venom I had given Vivian would have worn off in a couple hours, but Cain was going to need my blood to heal. My blood was the only antidote for my venom.

I chuckled as I held my head back and stretched my arms out on either side of me. It had been so long since I'd felt the power-hungry sensation that was coursing through me. Biting Vivian had sent me back to this place, but I'd been afraid of being reminded. Cain's fear, on the other hand, was potent. Looking down on him now, all I wanted was to see him suffer. I stooped down slowly, and he pulled away.

"The Queen will kill you for this!"

"I don't think so," I answered as I wiped at my mouth. "You missed the old me? Well, here he is, and he's grown impatient. You know how this works, Cain. Only my blood will heal you, and you have only minutes before my venom gets to your heart. That's when the real pain will start."

Cain hissed and pulled his hand away from his neck, sticky now with a yellow liquid. The veins covering my body faded, and color returned to my skin.

My eyes, however, remained red and fixated on Cain. Everyone was prey to me if I so wished, and he knew that. They all knew that.

"Tell me what you need the girl for, brother, or I'm going to let you die. And believe me, I'll sit here and smile as it happens."

Elinor

"Who was he?" Darian asked as we ran through the forest.

Cyrus and Skye were behind us, and so far, I didn't get the sense that we were being followed. "Who are you talking to?"

"Don't play dumb, Elinor. I'm talking about the vampire, the one who was with you the night of the attack. He remained close to the pack when you were unconscious, too. So, who is he? He's the one that warned you about the General, right?"

"And here I thought you were all muscle and no brain," I quipped, and he chuckled.

As much as we fought every chance we got, I knew Darian meant well. But now wasn't the time for explanations. We'd been running full-speed through the forest for twenty minutes now. Though we were outside our territory, we still needed to put more miles between us and our old home.

"I'll explain who he is once we're far enough away, okay? But yes, he was the one who told me about the General." We leaped over a fallen tree.

"Have you lost your mind? You're trusting a vampire?"

"A vampire who saved my life more than once and who helped to save Skye and my brother. Don't forget that," I said.

He didn't look pleased, but I didn't care. "So, you think

just because he did a few things to help you, he can be trusted?"

"Now isn't the time for this, Darian. Yes, he can be trusted. But you don't have to trust him. You just need to trust me."

He glanced at me then but said nothing because Cyrus suddenly pulled up beside me. "Stop."

We all stopped running, and he began turning in a circle. I tried to listen to the quiet forest. It didn't take long for the rest of us to both hear and smell the same thing he had.

"Vampires," Skye said.

Darian held out a bag with a few of my things to Cyrus. "Take Elinor and fly north. I'll catch up!"

"No," Cyrus and I said together.

Cyrus shook his head. "I can't leave Skye behind, and I can't carry them both."

I pointed my finger at Darian. "And I'm not leaving you behind to fight alone. You're the only one who knows where we're supposed to go."

Darian gritted his teeth as he stared off into the forest. My nose tingled with the nearing scent of the vampires. I couldn't tell many there were, but I couldn't leave Darian behind, even if he was a Guard.

"It's my job to protect you, not the other way around, Elinor. I promised your father—"

A lightning bolt struck me, sending Darian, Skye, and Cyrus flying backwards. My power awakened immediately, and I absorbed it. I looked down as the bolt danced over my arms and then seeped into my skin.

"I can protect myself, Darian."

The vampires and supernaturals we'd sensed earlier had finally caught up to us. I released the bolt I had consumed, hitting a witch in her chest. Thunder rumbled above us, and my power pulsed as if in response to it. Another bolt fell to the earth and then another, hitting a Bleeder and a male elf.

"Take Skye and leave!" I yelled at Cyrus as flames exploded from his hands to consume two Bleeders.

Darian shifted and tackled a Bleeder and an elf while Skye attacked a witch. Her sharp claws moved quickly, cutting the witch all over and preventing her from using her magic. Then she grabbed the witch's head with both hands and snapped her neck.

Cyrus's wings appeared, and he flapped them twice, creating a large wind that sent a few of our attackers to the ground. He grabbed Skye and flew off as Darian killed two Bleeders and a witch before they could get to their feet.

Targeting the witches and elves first was wise since their power could do more damage. I inhaled deeply, my eyes on a werewolf as he charged towards me. Darian rushed to my side and suddenly, we were surrounded by six Bleeders, an elf, a witch, and three werewolves.

My white eyes peered into Darian's black ones. "If I lose control, I need you to leave me. I'll be fine." He growled in protest, and I forced dominance into my next words. "Do as I say!"

He shook his head and lowered it, and I gathered my power at my center. My body was shaking as I tried to focus on nothing but what I was feeling and what I wanted to happen. Before we parted, Faelen had let me in on a secret— I'd been unconsciously training myself for this since I was a child. I wasn't a master at control, but I wasn't a novice either.

I focused on everything I had learned from Connor when he'd trained me for the Guards' examination. I inhaled sharply and ignored the creatures around me. When I exhaled, a clap of thunder echoed above us. Electricity charged the air as lightning bolts like whips appeared in both of my hands, and Darian and I turned our backs to each other.

The forest came alive with the sound of growls, howls, cracking lightning bolts, and cries of pain. Darian fought relentlessly, and I got to see firsthand why he was considered the best.

One of my whips wrapped around a werewolf in their final form, and my other whip came down hard on a Bleeder. The Bleeder fell to the ground, writhing in pain as I slapped it again and again.

I pulled on the whip around the werewolf's throat, tugging him to me. I released my other whip, and it vanished. Piercing the werewolf's chest with my claws, I shoved my hand inside him to grab his heart.

"I'm sorry," I murmured as I removed his heart with my hand, his pained howl burning itself into my mind.

This wolf had been someone's son, someone's husband, and maybe even someone's father. But now he was nothing but a mindless tool being used for someone's greed. I'm sure he would have thanked me for putting him out of his misery.

Suddenly, someone grabbed me from behind and threw me through the air. I hit the ground hard, skidding as I fell.

I winced, my teeth cutting my tongue when a tree trunk stopped me. But I got to my feet, despite the pain.

A female vampire, a Skin, was glaring at me with crimson red eyes. She hissed as she moved to attack me again, but quickly stepped back when I sent a bolt of lightning shooting out from my right hand and then my left.

I hadn't intended to do that, and both areas burned. My body was now shaking, my temperature increasing, and my wolf was clawing to be freed. I realized that if I shifted, I would lose any chance I had of maintaining control. It took a lot of strength to stay in final form. I swallowed the taste of blood in my mouth and clenched my jaw to hold myself back from shifting. If my tiny amount of control slipped, that would be it for me.

"I know everything," the vampire hissed, and I paused.

"What?"

She stood up straight and then spat on the ground between us. "I know everything about you and Will, you little werewolf whore! I saw the two of you tonight. I heard you as he fucked you. And now the Queen will know too—know that he's betrayed her!"

I swallowed hard, and she laughed. As she pushed back her tangled red hair, I realized that her scent was masked.

She began muttering to herself, clearly a little deranged. "I met Cain after I saw the both of you. I didn't tell him, though. No—" She began shaking her head wildly. "—I won't tell the Queen just yet. This can work in my favor." Then she broke out into another fit of laughter.

"I don't know what you think you saw or heard—"

"Don't you fucking speak to me as if I'm crazy! I know what I saw! I know what I heard! You! He picked you!" She moved to the side, crouching down as if to attack.

I winced as another bolt of lightning escaped my body. "Who are you?" I asked as I positioned myself into a fighting stance. I could tell she wasn't going to be easily beaten.

Maybe I'd have to shift after all. I had already told Darian what to do, and Cyrus and Skye were long gone. I didn't want to lose control, but Darian and I needed to get out of here.

A blur to my right caught my attention, and when I turned to look, my eyes fell on Will. He was covered in a yellow substance and blood, but he wasn't looking at me. He was staring at the woman in front of me.

"Don't," he told her, and her mouth stretched into a wide-set smile.

I was confused. Clearly, this vampire knew Will. But if

she had indeed seen us together, she'd have to die. She wasn't stable, that was clear. But Will looked nervous, fearful even. And he hadn't yet looked my way.

"Will, what's going on?" I inquired.

The woman's resounding laugh filled the space around us. "Tell her, Will. Tell your little pet who I am!"

Will didn't respond, but he finally looked my way. My brows pulled together at the regret in his eyes, and I started to panic.

"Okay, fine," the woman said. "If you don't tell her, I will! I'm his fiancée, wolf. I'm his fiancée, not you! I'm the one he goes home to after he's been with you!"

My scrunched-up face slowly smoothed out, my eyes darting from the redheaded vampire to Will. He said nothing to defend himself, and his silence only made the situation worse.

"Will? She's lying, right?" I asked, desperate for reassurance. He stepped forward, and I held my hand out to stop him. "Tell me. Tell me now that she's lying."

My wolf was howling loudly in my head, and a bolt of lightning traveled down my left arm to scorch the earth by my feet. The man I loved, the only man I'd ever given myself to, couldn't have a fiancée. Will would never have done that to me. I listened, desperately needing to hear him deny it. But when he spoke, I wished he hadn't.

"I can explain, Elinor. Listen to me . . ."

I couldn't hold back my power anymore. I felt a rope wrap around me, mentally yanking me back into myself. My eyes closed, and Will's words became muffled as I released my wolf and my power. All I heard was his pained cry as thunder like an explosion rattled the earth.

Then everything went black.

THE BLOODMOON WARS CONTINUES...

THE BLOODMOON WARS (A PARANORMAL
SHIFTER PREQUEL SERIES TO LUNA RISING)

The Revolution: Book 4 The Bloodmoon Wars (A Paranormal
Shifter Series Prequel to Luna Rising)

https://ssbks.com/BW4

So the vampire Queen was behind all the *disappearances* after all.

Will <u>SWEARS</u> to me he had no idea what his mother was doing

. . . but how can I trust him?

How am I to believe anything he says after being confronted by

. . . his fiancé?

Apparently, just because he loves me doesn't mean he feels the need to tell me the truth.

His endless secrets have my head spinning.

The only question is: when I kill the Queen with my newfound powers,

will he be my side?

. . . or hers?

https://ssbks.com/BW4

HAVE YOU READ THE FREE
BLOODMOON WARS PREQUEL?

https://ssbks.com/BWPrequel

Either my whole village dies... or I make the ultimate sacrifice.

As the son of our village's shaman, I'm expected to marry a

virgin bride. But I only have eyes for pregnant widow Ava, who is off-limits for me.

And because life isn't twisted enough, I get another curveball thrown at me...

Plagued by a dark vision, my father binds my soul to my body in an attempt to save me from the worst of what might await. But I'm not relying on a ritual to save myself--I'm going to find out what he saw... and stop it.

Soon I come to realize there's no way I'll get out of this mess alive.

When vampires attack our village, the vampire Queen offers me a terrible choice--one with implications for more than just the survival of Ava and the rest of my clan.

If I give into the Queen's demands, I'll spend an eternity of darkness at her side as the very thing I despise most. With everything and everyone I love at stake, I'd gladly give my life to save my village.

But can I condemn the rest of the world to the monster I'll become?

This is the prequel to the Bloodmoon Wars series.

Are you wondering how Will became a vampire? Click below to get your FREE copy of the The Dark Ages (Bloodmoon Wars Prequel)

https://ssbks.com/BWPrequel

ALSO BY SARA SNOW

THE LUNA RISING UNIVERSE

THE BLOODMOON WARS (A PARANORMAL
SHIFTER SERIES PREQUEL TO LUNA RISING)

The Dark Ages (Free Prequel)

https://ssbks.com/BWPrequel

The Awakening (Book 1)

https://ssbks.com/BW1

The Enlightenment (Book 2)

https://ssbks.com/BW2

The Revolution(Book 3)

https://ssbks.com/BW3

The Renaissance (Book 4)

https://ssbks.com/BW4

The New Age (Book 5)

https://ssbks.com/BW5

LUNA RISING SERIES (A PARANORMAL SHIFTER
SERIES)

Luna Rising Prequel (Free Download)

https://ssbks.com/LunaPrequel

Luna Rising (Book 1)

https://ssbks.com/LR1

Luna Captured (Book 2)

https://ssbks.com/LR2

Luna Conflicted (Book 3)

https://ssbks.com/LR3

Luna Darkness (Book 4)

https://ssbks.com/LR4

Luna Chosen (Book 5)

https://ssbks.com/LR5

THE VENANDI CHRONICLES

Demon Marked (Book 1)

https://ssbks.com/VC1

Demon Kiss (Book 2)

https://ssbks.com/VC2

Demon Huntress (Book 3)

https://ssbks.com/VC3

Demon Desire (Book 4)

https://ssbks.com/VC4

Demon Eternal (Book 5)

https://ssbks.com/VC5

THE DESTINE UNIVERSE

DESTINE ACADEMY SERIES (A MAGICAL ACADEMY SERIES)

Destine Academy Books 1-10 Boxed Set

https://ssbks.com/DA1-10

ENJOY THIS BOOK? I WOULD LOVE TO HEAR FROM YOU...

Thank you very much for downloading my eBook. I hope you enjoyed reading it as much as I did writing it!

Reviews of my books are an incredibly valuable tool in my arsenal for getting attention. Unfortunately, as an independent author, I do not have the deep pockets of the Big City publishing firms. This means you will not see my book cover on the subway or in TV ads.

(Maybe one day!)

But I do have something much more powerful and effective than that, and it's something those publishers would kill to get their hands on:

A <u>WONDERFUL</u> bunch of readers who are committed and loyal!

Honest reviews of my books help get the attention of other readers like yourselves.

If you enjoyed this book, could you help me write even better books in the future? I will be eternally grateful if you could spend just two minutes leaving a review (it can be as short as you like):

Please use the link below to leave a quick review:

https://ssbks.com/BW3

I LOVE to hear from my fans, so *THANK YOU* for sharing your feedback with me!

Much Love,

~Sara

ABOUT THE AUTHOR

Sara Snow was born and raised in Texas, then transplanted to Washington, D.C. after high school. She was inspired to write a paranormal shifter series when she got her new puppy, a fierce yet lovable Yorkshire Terrier named Loki. When not eagerly working on her next book, Sara loves to geek out at Marvel movies, play games with her family and friends, and travel around the world. No matter where she is or what she is doing, she can rarely be found without a book in her hand.

Or Facebook:
    Click Here
    https://ssbks.com/fb
    Join Sara's Exclusive Facebook Group:
    https://ssbks.com/fbgroup

Made in the USA
Columbia, SC
12 November 2021

48875347R00124